Published on behalf of Swindon Heritage by
The Hobnob Press,
8 Lock Warehouse, Severn Road, Gloucester GL1 2GA.

British Library cataloguing in publication data:
a catalogue record for this book is available from
the British Library.

Design and typesetting by Graham Carter.
Front cover art by Shannon Jones & Lydia Ponting.
Blueprints by Shannon Jones & Noel Ponting.

The text is set in Adobe Garamond Pro in 11pt/14pt.

ISBN 978-1-914407-22-2

This book is a not-for-profit project; any proceeds from its sale will be reinvested into other local history projects.

George Hobbs in his office in Swindon's GWR Works

Project: The Machine #2

Drawing Name:	*Vertical Elevation (landing configuration)*
Original Concept:	*Christopher Jackson*
Designers:	*James/Sandy/Paul*

1.	Magnetic flux
2.	Forward, retractable antenna (attraction mode)
3.	Fins (forward configuration)
4.	Bow cone containing motive batteries and guide beam receiver
5.	Forward Man Tunnel (entrance hatch) and airlock
6.	Forward store cabin
7.	Oxygen tank
8.	Alumite outer casing
9.	Silvered Mirror (main view screen)
10.	Combination Observation Room/Chart Room/Living Room
11.	Ball race for stabilisation mechanism of Observation Deck
12.	Aft Man Tunnel
13.	Hydrogen tank
14.	Aft cabin/washroom
15.	Motive batteries (aft)
16.	Fins fully extended in launchpad configuration
17.	Magnetic flux (repel mode)

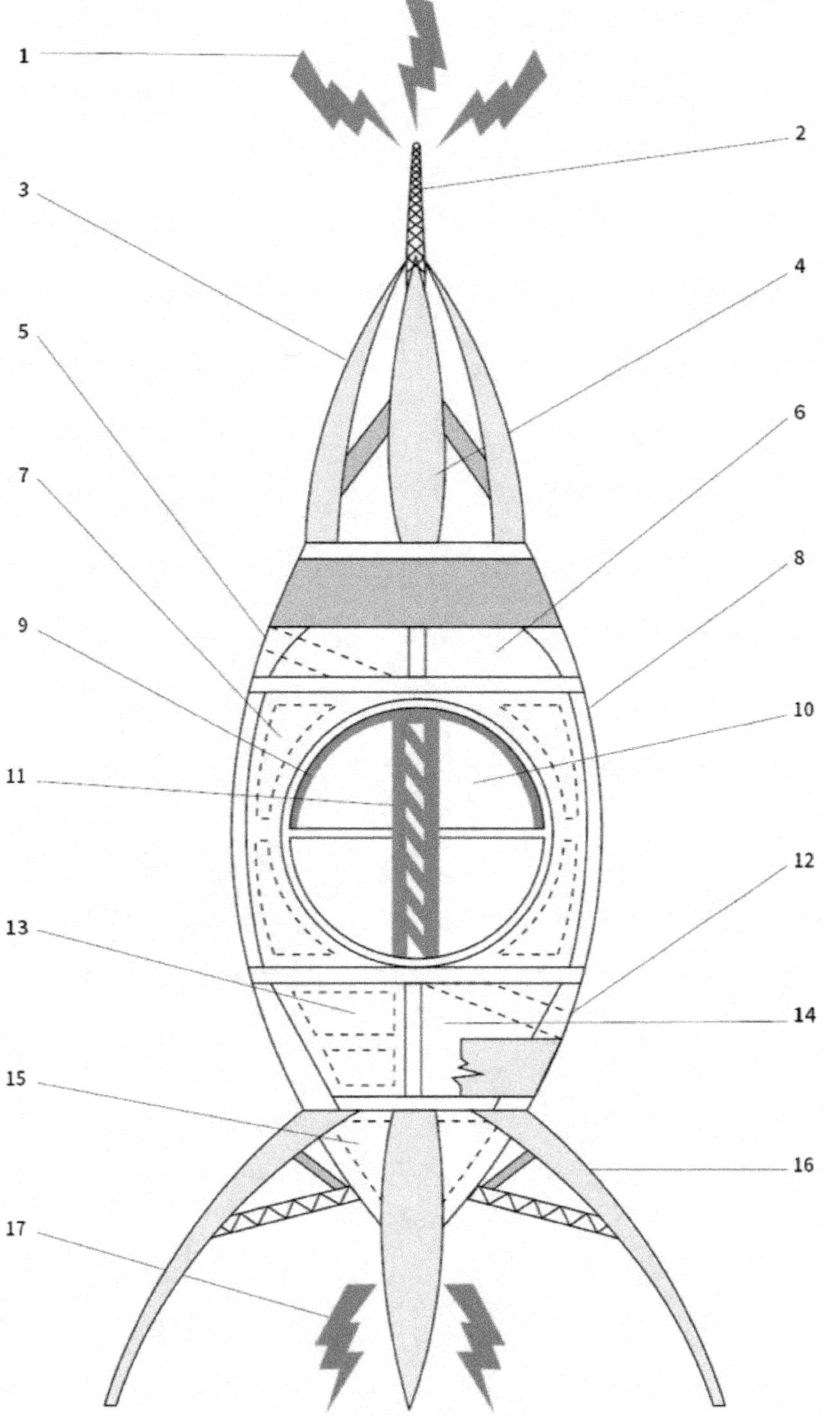
1
2
3
4
5
6
7
8
9
10
11
12
13
14
15
16
17

Introduction

By Noel Ponting & Graham Carter

Everything is becoming science fiction. From the margins of an almost invisible literature has sprung the intact reality of the 20th Century.
(JG Ballard, from Books and Bookmen, February 1971)

Sit down, strap yourself in – and prepare for launch! You won't be surprised to learn that our destination is going to be Venus – the clue is in the name – but there's much more to it than meets the eye.

For a start, what you are about to read was written in – wait for it – 1927, and even if that wasn't quite at the genesis of science fiction, it was certainly early enough in the development of the genre for *A Visit to Venus* to be a literary journey of discovery, as well as an inter-planetary one.

Its author, George Hobbs, wasn't a professional writer (although he undoubtedly had the talent to have been one); in his day job he was an important and respected Swindon railwayman, who spent much of his spare time reading and studying, and preaching his religious faith to others. Then, in the limited leisure time he had left, George put pen to paper, eventually writing hundreds of articles, across a phenomenally wide range of topics, which were published in the *Swindon Advertiser*, starting around the outbreak of the First World War and finishing at the outbreak of the Second.

We showcased many of his previously forgotten works in *A Swindon Wordsmith* (published in 2019), including his earlier forays into science fiction, while a follow-up book, *A Swindon Radical* (2021), includes yet more examples of his writing. The original intention was for the latter to include *A Visit to Venus*, but instead we decided to make it a companion book. Our main reason, we confess, was we think George would have been chuffed to see it produced as a separate book.

And, besides: we think it deserves to stand up on its own, especially when one considers *A Visit to Venus* was written so early in the development of science fiction that the rules of the game hadn't really been established yet, and George found himself having to invent the terms of engagement:

> I trust I do not weary the reader with too much detail in the construction of our machine. But as I feel sure there would have been many "whys" and "hows", with interjections suggesting doubt, if not of sheer unbelief had these details been omitted, I feel it incumbent upon me to tabulate them.

George is so early to the game, in fact, that he feels it necessary to offer a kind of apology to his readers for expecting them to believe it was possible for 'the machine' to travel at what then seemed the preposterous speed of 3,500mph. As if he had to excuse it. As if the creators of *Star Trek* would later have to justify Scotty's ability to defy the laws of physics while beaming people up and down from a planet's surface, or explain why most aliens encountered miraculoulsy speak English, or demonstrate the science behind the USS Enterprise's warp drives. George consequently gives us a description of his ship's propulsion method and reveals its secret to be not warp drives, but magnets.

As fantastical as he feared his story might sound to his contemporaries, the irony is that he completely underestimated the potential for rapid space travel; but how could even his fertile brain imagine that, 40 years later, Apollo 10 would set the record for human travel not at 3,500mph, but 24,791mph?

In some senses, then, George's approach can appear naïve to the modern eye, but there is a strong argument that his version of science fiction is nevertheless better by being purer than many of its 21st century counterparts. The modern reader, cinemagoer or Netflix subscriber could be excused for thinking that the genre is little more than a branch of the shoot-'em-up culture of computer gaming, since it largely relies on wall-to-wall action, explosions, cliffhangers and physical dilemmas, often drawing on predictable plots that are paper-thin, played out by characters who can be even thinner.

But *A Visit to Venus* boldly goes where only the best science fiction goes, generally avoiding melodrama, cliché and empty characters, and seeking out not just new worlds and new civilisations, but what the whole thing is ultimately about. Because, when you analyse it, good science fiction is not so much about what's *out there* as what's *inside us.*

As Captain James T Kirk and his crew discovered on their *Star Trek* adventures, exploring the final frontier ultimately told us far more about the human condition and our place in the universe than it did alien cultures. Otherwise, what would have been the point in going?

Admittedly, from time to time Kirk did take his shirt off for fisticuffs and a spot of swashbuckling, but he turned to violence only when forced to, and if he did employ his phasers, it was generally on 'stun' or as a last resort. In the end, it was all about finding out what his five-year mission taught us about life as we know it. And its successor, *The Next Generation*, was, if anything, even more of a study in human character and destiny, in which Captain Jean-Luc Picard was not only wiser than Kirk, but less inclined to taking his shirt off.

And so it is with *A Visit to Venus,* which uses space travel to transport its believable characters into moral dilemmas and philosophical issues, and – because George was a devout Christian with a mission to spread the word and find the truth – taking it one step further by making the story a theological adventure, too.

And we aren't done with parallels to *Star Trek* yet, including the coincidence that the main character (and the one who is writing the journey's journal) in *A Visit to Venus* (although not the *captain's* log) is known as Jim.

Also note how our author explores the moral questions the trip throws up by seeing how each new phase of the adventure is handled by the three crew members' different characters, attitudes and experiences – not least through Paul. George tells us Paul "can assemble his thoughts with coolness, with logic and with precision", and in heaping potentially emotional and emotive situations on cold characters like him, he is using exactly the same trick that gave us Spock in the original *Star Trek*, and Data in *The Next Generation.*

The half-human and half-Vulcan Spock was always torn between two cultures, ever susceptible to allowing his human emotion to overcome his alien logic, while Data, an android built by a human, was logical to a fault, but craved some of his maker's humanity.

In a similar fashion, when the originally cool, calculated and 'materialistic' Paul turns out to be more persuadable, hot-headed and passionate than we might have expected, George offers us a cultural reason for his different character: he's French!

By the way, there is another remarkable *Star Trek* coincidence in that Spock hailed from the planet Vulcan, and *A Visit to Venus* actually includes a reference to Vulcan – although not Spock's home planet, but rather the hypothetical planet of the same name that was once thought to orbit the sun, inside the orbit of Mercury (until it was disproved by Einstein's Theory of Relativity in 1915 and observations of the solar eclipse of 1919).

There is one more, crucial parallel with *Star Trek* because that saga – at least before its spin-off movies allowed it to degenerate into just another action film franchise – was the Prime Directive, the all-important first principle that the mission *could* not and *must* not, *under any circumstances*, interfere with the natural evolution of the civilisations they encounter. Remarkably, the same concept is found in *A Visit to Venus*; after our heroes' barbaric instincts cause an awkward intervention in Chapter 19, they have to be put right by their hosts, while the final chapters involve another, even more fundamental violation of the Venusian's Prime Directive: the kind of forbidden love interest that never seemed to stop Kirk!

Some of the results of George's crystal ball-gazing might raise some smiles among modern readers. For example, he wrongly concludes that space is 'no useless vacuum', and he introduces the somewhat charming idea that, one day, the likes of Vostok I and Apollo 11 might carry a supply of brandy for medicinal purposes! And while Kirk and Spock had their advanced communicators to stay in touch with each other, in *A Visit to Venus*, we find that poor Jim, Paul and Sandy have to make do with pocket mirrors for signalling!

But don't get the impression that *A Visit to Venus* is helplessly stabbing in the dark when it comes to technology – because, in other aspects, the author is spot-on.

For example, George's crew eat a kind of concentrated food that sounds remarkably like tonight's dinner on the International Space Station, and his ship has a device for seeing what's outside that is surely television – in an age when television was in its infancy, and George had probably not yet seen one.

And look out for some ideas that we think of as decidedly modern, such as vegetarianism – although, when they consider the morality of eating flesh in Chapter 19, our travellers stop short of (and do not even seem to have considered the concept of) veganism. On the other hand, the author's progressive and radical thinking is evident when his characters show a concern for each other's mental health that even the more enlightened in the 21st century are still only beginning to appreciate, while George tells us that the Venusians were also far too smart and advanced to believe in capital punishment, something that George wanted to see abolished, decades before it finally was.

But perhaps the most illuminating parallel between George's fiction and future events can be found in Chapter 5, because it seems to link to an event that took place 41 years after George put pen to paper.

It was arguably the most profound result of the entire moon-landing programme of the 1960s: a photograph taken by astronaut William Anders on Apollo 8, the first mission to leave Earth's orbit and travel to (although not land on) the moon. His famous but unplanned snapshot of the earth as it rose above the surface of the moon has made a lasting impact on humanity, not least because it emphasises the vulnerability of a planet threatened by climate change, and its impact was magnified because the photo was taken on Christmas Eve 1968. It is almost as if George can see that picture in his head when his characters take a look back, in awe, at the Earth:

> Best of all was the fact that the visional receiver transmitted upon the silvered mirror a clear reflection of objects in the surrounding space. Far, far away, the old Earth looked like a glorified moon, full orbed and majestic in its grand proportions... the Earth presented a picture of extreme fascination.

It's another indication that true science fiction and the best of the genre is ultimately to be found in those stories that reflect on where we have been and where we are, not just where we are going.

And it leads us to consider another mainstay of science fiction (and actual space travel): our obesssion with knowing if there is intelligent life on other planets.

But it's not our curiosity about the aliens that drives us, and whether they turn out out to be hostile or hospitable; all manifestations of science fiction are surely concerned with one thing in the long run: from the sorrow, seclusion and solitude of *2001: A Space Odyssey*, to Major Tom floating alone in his "tin can" in *Space Oddity*, and even to Elton John's rocket man "burning out a fuse up here, alone", it is ultimately about something far more terrifying than aliens and death rays: the loneliness and longing of human beings.

Make up your own mind, but it does seem to us that the ultimate point of *A Visit to Venus* is that same loneliness and longing.

As we have said, it was by no means George's first venture into the world of space fantasy and science fiction, although it was his longest and most ambitious. He had already written *The Mysterious Message* in 1922 and *A Visit to the Moon* in 1923. So *A Visit to Venus* is very much seen as a sequel to the latter and, as far as the genre is concerned, a worthy accompaniment to the former. Originally published in 26 chapters over 32 weekly instalments, we have made small adjustments to the format (but not the text, unless for clarity) to produce 32 chapters, numbered sequentially.

George's science fiction is further evidence of his willingness to embrace radical thought and ideas, regardless of the how this might be viewed by his contemporaries, particularly with regard to the more traditional elements within his congregation and readership. By 1927 he seemed to have little concern for how conservative elements in the Church received his new ideas. So, elsewhere in his writings, you will find numerous examples of him venting his frustration with Church elders in terms of its perceived, sclerotic attitude to falling attendances, and their failure to recognise that many younger members were already finding alternative forms of recreation.

But it is worth remembering that if George Hobbs was known for (and would have liked to be remembered for) anything, it was his mission to young people; they and his willingness to embrace changes for the better were his main concern. So how better to try to secure the future of the Church than to make it more engaging for its young adherents?

Besides, the wonders and the mystery of the solar system always fascinated him. He loved to lecture on the subject of astronomy to young peoples' fellowships, although, as far as we can tell, actual science fiction seems to have been reserved for the pages of the *Swindon Advertiser* alone.

We can only really guess as to what it was that inspired George to enter the genre in the first place. We might assume he read the seminal 1898 book *The War of the Worlds*, as well as *The First Men in the Moon* (1901) by HG Wells – an author, as it happens, who also became associated with the pacifism and internationalism that George championed in his own writing in the 1930s. And we know he was a reader of Sir Arthur Conan Doyle, someone who also flirted with science fiction, most notably with *The Lost World* (1912) and *The Poison Belt* (1913). Both these books, incidentally, featured a professor as one of the main characters, which is also the case in George's fantasy stories, *The Mysterious Message* (1922) and *Doctor Nickols – A Tale of Weird Happenings* (1923).

However, George felt compelled to issue the following disclaimer to accompany Part 1 of *A Visit to the Moon* in August 1923: 'In justice to everyone concerned, I also may state that I have never read any of the fiction writers upon this subject.'

This would seem to be at odds with the following, written 14 years later, which followed reports in the national press that showman scientist Professor Anthony MA had discovered a new British secret weapon referred to as a 'radio death-beam' (although actually strangely prescient of radar or sonar):

> Writers of "impossible" fiction of a decade ago, especially those of the Jules Vernes school, must soon be hailed as prophets and seers. They conceived the most fantastic "shape of things to come" and we, who read those things in our boyhood days, were told that we were perusing impossible trash.
>
> I remember reading as a youngster in one of those sensational periodicals published to stimulate the "manly" element in boys, of a scene which took place in a great fictitious battle.

> The captain of a British warship had on board a mysterious property unknown to any other Navy in the world. This was about to be utilised for the first time. In the cabin was an instrument before which sat the captain. By his side was a mirror into which he gazed with eager anticipation. The mirror was able to pick up and determine the range of any enemy warship within 15 miles. When the enemy ship passed into the field of view of the mirror the instrument sent out a death-dealing ray which blew up the ship and drowned the crew.
>
> I well remember how excited a friend and I were over this wonderful episode. We were very chagrined when we found that after all, what we had been reading was "simply fiction". While we had revelled in its wonderful presentation, our elders declared that it was all impossible and utterly foolish.

One further point to note is that Conan Doyle was one of the leading advocates of spiritualism, a movement that also held great fascination for George, and a metaphysical belief system to which, for a while anyway, he seemed wedded. Consequently, spiritualism makes an appearance in *A Visit to Venus*. In a section relating to the possible survivability of the soul after physical death, we get to hear of two female spirits that appeared to Paul, and this echoes a real-life experience that George himself recounted in his articles entitled *The Spirit World* and *The Revelation of Love*, in 1918.

And this surely links to another autobiographical element in the story: a reference to the fact that Louis Pasteur lost a child in infancy; George and his wife lost two.

But to return to possible inspiration for science fiction: this may have come from another place altogether. Unlike his mother-in-law, Eliza Thomas, who once boasted that she had never had any desire to attend such an establishment, George was, by his own admission, an avid cinemagoer. It's quite possible, therefore, that he saw the silent films *Le Voyage dans la Lune* (1902) and Fritz Lang's seminal *Metropolis*, released in 1927, the very same year that *A Visit to Venus* was written; clips from both films often appear in documentaries and in music videos to this very day.

But there may be one further source to consider. George's brother, William Hedley Hobbs, emigrated to the United States in 1909 with his wife (and two of her brothers), and it is already known that George was receiving publications such as *Reader's Digest* in the post, during the 1930s. *Amazing Stories*, hailed as the first American sci-fi magazine, was first published in 1926. Could it be that George received copies of these as well?

If he wasn't exactly ahead of the game, he was, at the very least, in the vanguard of British science fiction. To provide some further context: he was writing all this before *The Rocket to the Moon* by Thea von Harbou appeared in English as *The Girl in the Moon* (1930), and before the appearance in print of *Buck Rogers* (1929) and *Flash Gordon* (1934).

George lived and worked throughout the Second World War, and passed away somewhat prematurely on December 22, 1946, at the age of only 63. So, in what was to become the latter part of his life, he witnessed the deployment of V1 and V2 rockets over England, the early development of the jet engine and the dropping of the first atomic bombs on Japan. He would also have read of the capture of Wernher von Braun, and most likely lived just long enough to learn that von Braun and many of his former Nazi rocket engineers from Peenemünde were now working for the US Government at White Sands – the very people who would eventually spearhead the mission to put a man on the moon in 1969.

It is indeed a great shame that George appears to have ceased contributing to the Advertiser in 1940 because (and to quote from his obituary) 'during the war years [he] had to reduce his outside activities in order to keep pace with the extra work that arose'. If only he had been spared his final illness and taken up the pen with a vengeance once again; goodness knows what he would have made of it all.

When *A Visit to Venus* first appeared in the *Swindon Advertiser* on January 7, 1927, George pointed out that writers of contemporary science fiction often tended towards Mars as the planet of choice, but he would be different, choosing Venus instead, and when he wrote a factual article about the planets in 1938 (reproduced in *A Swindon Radical*), he informed us:

> When I wrote my fantasy, "A Visit to Venus", which appeared in the columns of "The Swindon Advertiser" as a serial, I found this planet an excellent subject upon which to base that story. I took advantage of all that was known about her and called upon my imagination to fill in the details.

In fact, contemporary knowledge (or rather: the lack of it), allied to popular culture, made Venus the obvious choice, its mysteriousness and its mythology fitting the storyline perfectly. It was anyone's guess what was behind Venus's unchanging white clouds, which are impenetrable by visual telescopes, but the classical persona was an optimistic one that imagined the planet as a bringer of peace. Even long after George died, reputable astronmers were still speculating that beneath its steely facade, there might be some kind of tropical paradise awaiting potential visitors.

In fact, when it was finally visited by Russian and American probes in the late 1960s, Venus proved to be more or less the opposite to the heavenly place imagined by George and others; the surface temperature is upwards of 460°C, the pressure is high enough to crush rocks, and it rains acid.

As Professor Brian Cox pointed out in notes accompanying a performance of *The Planets* by Holst, rather than being a kind of heaven, 'Venus is a vision of hell.' But he also noted that, perhaps two billion years ago, 'Venus may once have been temperate, life-supporting perhaps, with rivers and oceans and blue skies.' So pretty close to the Utopia that George imagined, even if Cox concluded that Holst's Venus movement was 'a requiem for a failed planet'.

But don't let that put you off. We're heading to Venus regardless, and it is thanks to George that we know what our spaceship looks like. His pen picture has enabled us to not only produce a 'blueprint' of 'the machine', but also adopt the style of later science fiction comics and books to produce our cover (with apologies to *Amazing Stories*).

So climb on board, throw the forward control to full power, brace yourself for a rollicking good read and prepare for... A Visit to Venus.

Special *INTERPLANETARY ISSUE*

A VISIT TO VENUS

January 7th 1927

2d

STORY BY GEORGE E. HOBBS

Chapter 1

How often has that trite saying, "It is the unexpected which happens," been verified in human experience? That which is unthinkable to-day is the fact of experience to-morrow. A dreamer allows his imagination to run riot. He dreams the abnormal, and lo, in a short decade, the seemingly grotesque phantasm has crystallised into actuality.

Men laugh, men sneer, men hold up hands in pious horror, but that does not prevent things happening nowadays. Galileo propounded his theory of the solar system, and all the recantations in the universe could not disestablish progressive truth. It was flagrantly "impossible", but who outside a mental institute would dare to say the sun was subservient to the Earth? The steam and electric locomotive, the heavier-than-air machine, the submarine, wireless telegraphy and telephony were all impossible, or were they inventions of his Satanic Majesty?

Yet these things are not only established facts, but are commonplace in the tide of human affairs. And cannot other things be possible too, the possibility of achievements at present so logically illogical as to border on the ridiculous?

But, a visit to Venus? A visit with such a sequel, that, if true, must revolutionise all subsequent thinking, and postulations.

Such were some of the thoughts that coursed through my mind as I sat and gazed at a pile of MS [manuscript], in front of me. Far into the night had I sat and read the story contained therein. It was seemingly preposterous and unthinkable. A phantasy written by an unbalanced mind. And yet, in the face of past achievements (achievements brought to fruition by harnessing the sciences, physical and psychical, dare I say?), it was preposterous and unthinkable!

In the grey of the dawn I turned into bed, but such was the effect of that pile of MS, I found sleep to be impossible.

Then I came to a definite decision. I remembered the journal of my late friend, Christopher Jackson. He claimed to have visited the moon, and though the claim seemed past belief, I published his story to the world. I determined, therefore, after wooing refreshing sleep, to review the latter part of his journal and compare it with the MS before me. If then I was satisfied that the present claim would bear production, I would publish this also to the world. Having reached this decision, I was enabled to rest my mind and enjoy a refreshing sleep.

Later in the day, I took the journal of my late friend and began a task, the result of which is now placed before the reading public.

One thing only would I say as a preface to the remarkable story I am about to relate. My position is simply that of narrator to the claims contained in the MS. I make no statement of belief or unbelief.

First, then, it seems imperative that I traverse a little of my late friend's journal. I do this in order to make the sequence more clear to those who did not read *A Visit to the Moon*.

My friend, Christopher Jackson, had long cherished a belief that, given a properly constructed machine, he could visit our satellite, the moon. Believing his idea practicable, he constructed a machine with the assistance of three deaf-mute companions. Upon the completion of the machine (one that was unique in every detail), he journeyed alone to the moon. After passing through some interesting experiences amongst the Lunarians, he came back to the Earth, wrote up his journal, and deposited it with me. The contents of that journal I published through the medium of the Swindon Advertiser.

The concluding paragraph of the journal was as follows:

> There is little more to add. I have been back upon the Earth about three months. I found my three deaf-mute friends had calculated an approximate date for my return. But it was one month after that date when I descended into their camp. They are here now with my machine snugly hidden. I shall not name the place in my journal, but shall give the geographical position only by word of mouth to my friend. If I live, I shall return again to the moon, when I hope my friends will accompany me.
>
> Christopher Jackson

In publishing this remarkable story, I appended this explanatory note: "I have faithfully given to the world the details of my friend's journal. I cannot vouch for the accuracy of his claim. I could only do as I have done – record his journal.

One thing could have established his claim, but unfortunately that proof is impossible of production. My friend died before he could tell me the location of his machine. The deaf-mutes may know of my existence, but even then they would not betray my friend's secret without his consent. That permission cannot now be given. What those three friends will do, I have no knowledge. Probably they will journey to the moon themselves. If they do, the probability is we shall hear later of their exploit. Until then I can say no more."

And so I thought the matter ended.

Imagine my surprise, therefore, when I found myself in the receipt of a remarkable sequel. It was none other than a claim that the three friends had actually visited the planet Venus. The claim in itself is truly remarkable, but the further statements as to the sentient life upon the planet, their constitution and economy, is contrary to all past speculations. But I must not anticipate. I must tell the story in coherent sequence.

Writers of fiction, when dealing with the subject of adventures upon other planets, invariably fix the venue of activity upon the planet Mars – our nearest outside neighbour. This attitude is consistent with logic, for the physical economy of that planet ever invites the imagination to run a riotous course. But the imagination is not so profoundly stirred when thinking of the planet Venus – our nearest inside neighbour.

In the eye of the telescope the topography of Mars changes with the seasons. That of Venus seems eternally to remain fixed. The axial revolutions of Mars are known to the very second. That of Venus seems still controversial.

Mr WF Denning, FRAS, says of Venus:

> As a telescopic object, it must be confessed that Venus is disappointing. Her lustrous aspect encourages an expectation which is far from being realised. The white disc, free from obvious detail, such as that which diversifies Mars and Jupiter, does not call for interested study, though, if the planet be crescented, the picture is a very attractive one and gratifies the eye. The student, however, is apt to tire of a similarity of aspect. It is the study of detail and of changes in the forms and motions of features which so pleasantly maintain the interesting planetary work and furnishes results which are important.

It can readily be seen, therefore, that Venus is a disappointing subject for romance. If the surface of Venus was but exposed to the extent of Mars, or to that of the moon, romancers long ere this would have devoted some of their writings to adventures upon this planet. No such effort, to my knowledge, has ever been attempted, and therefore the contents of this journal must be unique.

Without more preamble, I will [return] to my task, again reminding the reader that in recording this story, I subscribe no comment upon its claims. At the same time, I count it an honour in being the means by which the contents of this journal are made known to the world.

Chapter 2

It was quite in the order of things for the journal to be prefaced with an explanatory covering letter. It was rather voluminous in detail and I have abridged it to meet the needs only of proper sequence. The letter reads as follows:

> Dear Sir – I have little doubt but that an agitated surprise will be your chief emotion when you open and peruse the enclosed manuscript. Nevertheless, I trust that its contents will be received and dealt with in the same sympathetic manner as was the journal of my late chief, Christopher Jackson.
>
> First, there are one or two things I must make clear to you.
>
> There were three of us in the retinue of our chief, and I shall introduce the three by Christian name only. Paul, a Frenchman; Jock, a Scotsman, known to us by the more familiar sobriquet of 'Sandy'; and myself, James.
>
> It may sound strange to you that we were 'known' to each other by these names, seeing that our late chief gave you to understand we were deaf-mutes. Also, he gave you to understand we were blood brothers. Mr Jackson simply gave you information which he himself believed to be true. We had no wish to criminally deceive him, seeing that he was ever a kind and considerate friend. By some strange physiological phenomenon, we each bore facial resemblance to the other. For this reason we agreed to be a blood

brotherhood, and seeing we were 'mutes', this difficulty was not great. For reasons that in no way concern this narrative, our policy of rigid silence was actuated purely from expediency... We were fully acquainted with all the details of our late chief's journey to the moon... Hearing of his death we mutually agreed to reconstruct the machine upon more ambitious lines and set our course for the planet Venus... Our adventures are fully set out in the journal.

In conclusion, I may add that Jock was chosen as leader of the expedition, while I became its chronicler.

Signed on behalf of the expedition, JAMES

One word more would I say before recording the contents of this remarkable journal. It is written in the form of a log or diary. I, however, shall write the contents as a connected story, giving dates only occasionally.

It was on 23 October, 19– we expected to witness the return of our chief from his visit to the moon. The machine was so constructed that we had little doubt of the success of his venture. It was on 22 November 19– when he descended into our camp. As he stepped out of the machine, our demonstrations of joy were almost instantaneously suppressed by the appearance of his features. He was deathly pale and showing every sign of complete prostration. The sight of his faithful retainers may have acted upon him like an enervating tonic. His pale face lit up with a smile. With a hand grip all round, he signed to us that his journey had been a complete success.

Feverishly he wrote up the account of his adventures, and each of us, in turn, read that wonderful story.

Towards the completion of his writing, Paul and I were, one evening, taking our usual patrol around the camp. Seeing the coast clear, Paul whispered his fears to me concerning the state of Mr Jackson's health. Those whispered fears startled me considerably. I could depend upon Paul's verdict of the case. He would have gone far in the medical profession but for an unfortunate circumstance which compelled him to leave France.

"Jim," he whispered, "the chief will be dead in a month. I thought at first his condition was due to the high tension he had been living under, throughout his wonderful trip. But I am certain, now, he has organic trouble, which must eventually prove fatal. His dogged determination to complete his journal is the only thing keeping him alive, just sheer force of will. When that is achieved and he has placed the story in the hands of some mutual friend, he will collapse."

And so it proved to be. Just four days over the prescribed month, we heard of his death. Seeing we should no longer have his valued help and companionship, we mutually agreed upon a reconstruction of a machine of our own. Long and earnestly we talked the matter over and finally decided to make an attempt to reach the planet Venus. I believe I am correct in saying no previous attempt has ever been made to reach this wonderful planet.

I would have the readers of this journal appreciate at this point the difference between our contemplated venture and the venture of our late chief, not by the comparisons which are ever odious, but by other measures which tabulate the difference of construction, economy, distance and period of the two enterprises.

When Mr Jackson undertook his journey to the moon, we constructed a machine for his needs only. The storage tanks into which oxygen was pumped under high pressure, were only of sufficient capacity for the needs of one. As the journey to and from the moon would be, in round figures, 500,000 miles, and a stay of one month upon the lunar surface, we calculated a period of nine months.

But with our present project, the capacity of the machine, in every detail, would have to meet the needs of three. The period of absence would also be much extended. Instead of a journey consisting of a half-million miles, our contemplated venture would embrace no less than 50 million miles. But as the journal will prove, we ventured in the face of almost overwhelming odds – and we achieved.

The reader will naturally expect a detailed account of our machine. As we wish for the fullest publicity – save in those details which are technical secrets – those details may be tabulated.

The outer casing of the machine was made from an alloy which is the profound secret of the syndicate. We named it "alumite". To the technical reader, I may say that alumite has a specific gravity of 1.94 against that of 2.56 for aluminium (Mr Jackson's machine was made from the latter metal). In shape, the longitudinal section was elliptical, the cross section being a perfect circle. At each end of the ellipse, an extended cone was secured in which were housed our motive batteries. Two feet from the outer shell, an inner case was built. It was cylindrical in design, with ends dished inward, and with the central portion of the body a perfect sphere. It was so designed in order to secure the maximum space between the casings for the storage of oxygen. The inner shell was rigidly secured to the outer case by means of transoms made of alumite.

Inside the central spherical portion of the inner shell, the combination observation, chart and living room was constructed. This combination room was free from all contact with the inner case, except on the horizontal plane, where two gimbals found almost frictionless motion in a ball race. There was an obvious need for keeping the observation room perfectly poised. When rising upon the initial flight, the machine would be upon an inclined plane upwards; upon reaching the gravitational zone of Venus, the machine would be upon an inclined plane downwards; while, between the two gravitational zones, the machine would ride upon an even keel. In effect, the course of the flight would resemble a huge arc.

Chapter 3

Seeing that we should be enclosed within the chart room, the intelligent reader will naturally wish to know what means we had at our disposal for true observation. We had no windows, as was the case with the machine of Mr Jackson.

Immediately in front of the ingress and egress man-tunnel, and completely circling the machine, a visional receiver was fixed. Inside the receiver, a series of transverse wires converged to a common centre. Each individual wire was capable of receiving objective vibratory impressions, somewhat on the same principle as an aerial receives the etheric vocal and instrumental disturbances from a broadcast station. In our experiments we had discovered, whether an object was in motion – such as a bird or aeroplane, or stationary – such as a building, hill or tree, each individual object, by its electronic constitution, constantly projected vibratory emanations. Such a discovery entirely eliminated the use of windows and the more unsatisfactory periscope. The objective vibrations collected at the common centre of the receiver and were transmitted to the chart room. Here they were projected upon a large mirror, made of highly polished silver.

Another feature of interest was our super-high-power combination wireless set. It was unique in every detail, and far surpassed any previous idea. The reader must bear with me when I say that this invention is the secret of the syndicate; I must refrain from a detailed description. I may, however, say this: we had a specially constructed director which enabled us to definitely control the path of etheric disturbance. The usual effect of disturbance produced from a broadcast station is circular expansion; or, I suppose it would be more correct to say globular expansion. The path of disturbance is really an ever-expanding globe, moving with the velocity of light.

With our director we could broadcast or receive either to or from the Earth or Venus. For obvious reasons, while we intended to receive from the Earth, we should make no attempt to broadcast. At the same time, should there be sentient beings upon Venus, we hoped to detect their existence long before we reached that planet.

Our food supply, of which we took a three years' stock, was in concentrated form. This was stored in a room in the fore part of the machine, between the chart room and the dished end of the inner shell.

In Mr Jackson's voyage to the Moon he found by practical experience certain features of his appointments to give the highest satisfaction. The principle of these features we decided to embody in our present project.

As there will be readers of this narrative who did not read of this wonderful achievement, I may be permitted to give a few details of their construction.

On the outer casing, atmospheric gauges were placed. From the gauges, running through the oxygen tanks, connections engaged with automatic release valves in the chart room. The working arrangement was of a very simple character. As the mercury fell in the gauges (which, of course, we knew would occur when passing out of the Earth's atmospheric belt), the automatic valves would release to us in the chart room the precious, life-restoring oxygen. With the fall of the mercury to zero, the maximum oxygen would be released.

An indicator in the chart room governed by the velocity of escaping oxygen, by inverting action, indicated atmospheric density. When the valves were closed the indicator recorded 14.7lbs. atmospheric pressure. But when the velocity of escaping oxygen was at its highest, the indicator recorded zero. By this means we knew we should be able to check Mr Jackson's data of atmospheric pressures.

I trust I do not weary the reader with too much detail in the construction of our machine. But as I feel sure there would have been many "whys" and "hows", with interjections suggesting doubt, if not of sheer unbelief had these details been omitted, I feel it incumbent upon me to tabulate them.

I trust that the most interesting feature of this narrative will be the account of the actual voyage with its many adventures and discoveries. But in the meantime, here's a word or two in reference to our motive power.

The principle of our motive force was identical to that of Mr Jackson's. In point of fact it was his invention – or discovery – purely. And here I am faced with some difficulty. As we of the expedition wish to honour the memory of our late chief, and as we wish not to betray more of his secret than he himself would have done, I will describe the motive power in his own words, taken from his log.

> My motive power was situated in the extreme end of the pear-shaped appendages [corresponding in our machine to the extended cone ends], and was designed to throw out, from either end, powerful magnetic antennae. It was so arranged that from a deflection indicator in my observation room, I could at will reverse the poles of attraction and repulsion. When commencing the upward flight, the fore part of my machine became charged with a magnetism hitherto unknown. I have named my discovery "Local velocified magnetism".
>
> By the aid of multiple intensifiers, so compact as to occupy but a cubic foot of space, I was able to throw out magnetic [flux from the] antennae forty million times the length of my machine. And here lay my secret – I could localise, or isolate this power within any required diameter. That is to say, I could throw out this wonderful force on a 240,000 mile line, having a radius of influence not greater than four feet. It was as though my machine could slip into a tube and be conveyed to the Moon within its solid walls. So localised was the magnetic influence that a compass placed six feet away on either side of my machine remained unaffected.
>
> At the same time, in the appendage at the base (the aft part of our machine), I was able to set up repulsion, which gave me, after several experiments, more power than I needed to resist terrestrial gravitation. When, therefore, the Moon was in a favourable position for my flight, I should have a 'pull' from our satellite and a 'push' from the Earth.

The foregoing, as I intimated, was taken from Mr Jackson's log, through a real desire to perpetuate his memory by his invention. But seeing we had to negotiate a distance over one hundred times the distance of the Moon, it can readily be appreciated the motive power had to be very much intensified. Adopting Mr Jackson's idea of multiple intensifiers, we found, by simple calculation, the power needed for our enterprise. Having found that power, we proved its stability by a definite process of indication.

But now another problem presented itself. With the increase of attractive power in the fore battery, we had also to intensify the aft battery for repulsion. The combined power gave us a velocity of 3,500 miles per hour. This speed was much too high for the initial flight (the reason I will indicate in a moment), but just how to obviate the difficulty caused us some worry.

We eventually overcame the difficulty by inserting an apparatus which reversed the poles in the aft battery, transforming the negative into a positive action. By this means we could brake down our speed to that which was required.

The speed may be thought to be truly amazing, as indeed it is compared with ordinary standards. No method of mechanical impulsion or propulsion can ever hope to attain anything like this velocity. It can only be achieved by the method I have already briefly indicated.

Rapid as our flight would be, no harm could possibly come to the machine while travelling through the attenuated etheric space outside the Earth's atmospheric belt. But to attempt such a high velocity through the belt – short as the flight would be – would spell disaster. At the same time we wished to travel easily at the commencement in order to check Mr Jackson's observations upon the depth and density of the Earth's atmospheric belt.

With the completion of the machine we spent five days in an exhaustive test of the oxygen chamber. We could not afford to have even the smallest escape of this precious gas.

We had little to no knowledge of the physical conditions prevailing upon the planet Venus. It may contain an atmosphere so attenuated as to be fatal without respiratory appliances. On the other hand, it may approximate to that of our Earth. We did not know. It was therefore incumbent upon us to make provision for every possible contingency.

In the fullness of time the machine was completed and provisioned to the satisfaction of each member of the expedition. How fully could we enter into the emotions of our late chief as he reached the final hour preceding his voyage over an unknown track. Emotions now thrilled our beings to the very core. We were setting out to achieve, or...

No! We would not think of defeat. In a few short hours we should commence a voyage of discovery, a voyage of adventure!

Chapter 4

It was a decidedly recondite problem that faced us when working out the right moment for our initial flight. Briefly I may state it here.

The planet Venus completes 13 revolutions around the Sun to that of 8 revolutions for the Earth. As both orbits are eccentric, it follows that only on rare occasions the two planets approach to their nearest distance. With Venus at superior conjunction, a distance of 160 millions of miles separate the Earth from the Goddess of Love: but when she is at inferior conjunction, a distance of only 26 millions of miles is recorded. Approximately every nineteen months, Venus is at inferior conjunction to the Earth.

Our machine was completed by 2 November, 19–, and we found that Venus would be at inferior conjunction on 15 December, 19–, about six weeks later. At the same time, we knew that travelling 3,500 miles per hour, the journey would occupy about ten months. As the magnetic antennae were designed to "grip" the planet at its conjunction distance, it follows that Venus, ten months afterwards, would be hopelessly out of position. We therefore had to decide upon a bold plan of action.

When Venus was at inferior conjunction, we decided to throw out the forward antennae, commence our flight, and when in the apparent void between the two planets, permit Venus to "drag" our machine with her upon her orbital journey. Having made up our minds upon a definite course of action, we awaited the time for the initial flight with high hopes for a successful venture.

We made the camp snug against inquisitive visitors, and at 8pm on 15 December, 19–, we entered the machine.

Our first care was to see that the cap covering the man-tunnel was securely fastened, and the jointing band airtight. Then, after an inspection of the food cabinet, we entered the chart room and closed the sliding panel. All was now ready for the start.

At 10pm – the moment of right conjunction – Sandy threw the forward control into contact at full power. As the magnetic antennae moved with the velocity of light, we calculated it would take about two and a half minutes for them to reach the planet Venus. During that period, while Sandy was watching the indicator of the forward control, Paul stood ready to switch in the aft control in its positive action. Slowly I counted off the seconds of the last half minute. At two minutes and nineteen seconds, we felt a movement of the machine. Immediately Paul threw in the aft control, and magnificently the machine rose into the air. Our journey, with its dangers, its adventures, and its wonderful possibilities, had commenced.

Having given the reader a full and detailed account of the construction of our machine, and the commencement of the voyage, I now propose to record our subsequent progress in a more pleasing form. That is in the form of a story narrative.

"Now we will check the chief's figures," said Sandy, as the machine rose into the air. "Jim, get out the log-book from the inner locker, there's a good fellow, and jot down the readings as Paul calls them out. I will watch the controls for a while."

Before the commencement of the voyage, while the machine still nestled upon the struts, the mercury stood in the columns of the gauges at thirty inches. This, of course, meant that the mercury balanced 14.7lbs per square inch atmospheric pressure.

The journey had scarcely commenced when Paul spoke.

"The mercury is falling rapidly, Jim," said he. "Our altitude is five miles and the mercury is down 16½ inches. Thank God the release valves are working perfectly, for I began to find the air somewhat oppressive."

And so I tabulated the figures as Paul called to me. In a moment or so he called to me again in disjointed sentences: "Altitude, 10 miles; mercury, 23.6 inches – not falling so rapidly now – altitude 100 miles – 250 miles – zero! We are out of the belt now! Hurrah! Away now on to Venus!"

So perfect had been the adjustment between the fore and aft controls, we were able to keep the machine upon a steady 200 miles per hour speed. It had, therefore, taken us but one hour and a quarter to clear the belt. Once out of the belt, Sandy reversed the poles of the aft battery, thereby setting up repulsion.

With the forward control at full attraction and the aft control at full-powered repulsion, our machine literally shot forward to the maximum velocity of 3,500 miles per hour.

"Well," said Sandy, after seeing that the machine was riding steadily upon an even keel, "so far as we can conjecture, we need fear no danger until our approach to the gravitational zone of Venus. Then we shall have to exercise every caution. But that is some months away."

"Yes, that's so," replied Paul thoughtfully. "But I was just wondering if, after all, we ought not to set regular watches. Not so much to be on the alert for danger, seeing, as you say, we are fairly safe for some months, but rather that each in turn will be on observational duty throughout the whole voyage. Still, you are the boss, Sandy. What your commands are will be obeyed."

"What do you think of Paul's suggestion, Jim?" asked Sandy.

"I think it a good one," I replied. "You select the periods and we stand by your ruling."

"Very good. Then I will take the first period of eight hours, you take the second eight, Jim, and Paul the third eight. We will follow in that order until we reach the gravitational zone of our objective. But, first of all, as everything seems to be in order, just compare your figures with the readings of the chief. I'd like to see how they agree."

Before I could lay the two log books upon the table for comparison, an exclamation from Paul brought Sandy and I to his side.

"The chief was right after all!" said he, excitedly. "I doubted his statement that an æther of measurable density pervaded the whole universe. Do you both remember? The chief recorded in his log he had a constant half an inch of mercury in the gauge when he went on his voyage to the moon, I honestly confess I doubted it! But it's true! We are well out of the belt and the gauges stand steady at half-an-inch. It is just as the chief stated. There is no ætherless space! No useless vacuum! But a connecting medium of life to every planet and to every sun!"

Truly wonderful was this confirmation of Mr Jackson's data, bringing with it again a direct refutation of the old popular belief. Silently we stood and watched the indicator. No variation occurred, and I may say here that the half-an-inch stood constant throughout the whole voyage. It proved to us beyond the shadow of a doubt throughout universal space there was an æther of measurable density.

We found, too, that our record of the Earth's atmospheric belt approximated to that of Mr Jackson's record. Five miles above the Earth's surface we found the pressure to be 7.39lbs per square inch, to that of 7.35lbs in Mr Jackson's log. At ten miles' altitude our readings gave us 3.2lbs against that of 3lbs in Mr Jackson's reading. In each case we found our figures to so nearly agree with his that the differences were negligible.

We were greatly pleased at the accord of our several independent readings. For, although Paul expressed a passing doubt respecting ætheric density between the planets, generally we had explicit faith in the integrity of Mr Jackson's records. It also ought to have some weight with the reader of this journal emphasising the accuracy of the data obtained.

Placing the log book upon the table, I indulged in a luxurious stretch. So far as I was concerned, I began to feel the need of mental and physical rest.

"Tired?" queried Paul, with a smile.

"I am that," I answered. "We have been busy for the past twenty hours almost without pause, and I for one could do with a few hours' rest."

"That's right, boys, have your rest," responded Sandy. "I'll call you, Jim, when my watch is up. You had better take some food first. I could do with..."

What Sandy "could do with", and whether his desire was satisfied I did not know for some hours. I was fast asleep upon the chart room floor.

Chapter 5

It seemed to me I had scarcely closed my eyes when I found myself vigorously shaken.

"Wake up!" said a voice which I certainly did not recognise.

"I don't want to wake up," I answered irritably. "I want to have my sleep out."

"Sleep out! Why, man, you've been raising the very devil with your unholy snoring for the past seven hours. Come on and take your watch." And I arose to find Sandy with a smile upon his face and a weary look in his eyes.

"I'm sorry, old man," said I, now thoroughly awake. "I thought I had just closed my eyes when you called me. Get yourself in the bunk and I'll take the watch."

May I digress here and refer to one aspect of our domestic arrangement with which I have not previously dealt. It will occur to the reader the utter impossibility of continuing ten months without some means of washing. A swill in cold water is necessary and beneficial. Obviously, we could not carry tanks of water. Our method was very simple. We carried two tanks of hydrogen gas in the aft part of the machine, between the dished end of the inner shell and the chart room. Here was situated our washing place.

A tube led from the hydrogen tanks to a mixing bulb, fixed about 8 feet from the wash-bowl. The bulb was made from "Alumite", with walls 3/8 inch thick.

It was so made to withstand the explosive shock when combining with the oxygen – the combination being effected by means of a sparking arrangement from the aft control. The right proportion of gas was, of course, governed by finely adjusted automatic release valves. Passing out of the mixing chamber, the water passed through a "chill" grid in order to render it ice cold, and thence to the wash bowl. After use, the water was cleansed and passed back into a converter, separating the constituent gases and returning each to its respective tank.

I enjoyed that first dowse in clear cold water, and, feeling refreshed, I went again into the chart room and began my observational duties.

We had now been on our voyage for twelve hours and had journeyed nearly 40,000 miles. The machine was behaving splendidly, and the oxygen supply was good and sufficient. In fact, the quality of the air was such that one may have imagined oneself upon some promontory, breathing the pure ozone from the sea.

Best of all was the fact that the visional receiver transmitted upon the silvered mirror a clear reflection of objects in the surrounding space. Far, far away, the old Earth looked like a glorified moon, full orbed and majestic in its grand proportions. In our journey we could not hope to see the Earth in crescent – as Mr Jackson saw her when on his voyage to the moon. When our late chief went to the moon, our satellite was full orbed, therefore he had the Earth between himself and the sun. Our journey was towards the sun, therefore it was impossible to see the Earth in crescent. Nevertheless, the Earth presented a picture of extreme fascination. I could detect with perfect ease the continental areas, revealing to me that the hemisphere towards me enjoyed a cloudless sky.

The hours of my watch passed rapidly. Every moment was full of an ever-growing wonder and delight. Eventually I roused up Paul, and after taking a light repast of concentrated food and drink, I sought again my bunk for rest.

Our first trouble came some hours later, and never shall I forget the thrill of horror that pulsed through my being. Even with the plans that are most carefully laid, there is always the contingency of the unexpected. Sometimes the error is of a glaring nature. Too much has been taken for granted; the apparent lesser has been ignored in face of the apparent greater. And then it may be found that the apparent lesser was the greater, and disaster is the inevitable result.

But enough of moralising. The fact was we had forgotten one possible contingency – the near proximity of the moon.

Paul had just entered the forward store cabin in order to obtain a fresh supply of food, when a startled cry escaped his lips. I was writing up the log at the table and Sandy was bending over me, reading through what I had written. Hastily we turned at the sound of his startled exclamation, and to our dismay saw that the doorway of the fore cabin, which should be in alignment with the doorway of the chartroom when the machine was upon an even keel, had almost disappeared from my view. We knew at once that some influence had deflected our machine.

"What the devil's amiss?" exclaimed Sandy in the stress of his excitement.

"Look in the mirror!" I cried. "Great heavens, Sandy, we are descending upon the moon. Fools that we were not to have foreseen this possibility!"

The sight that revealed itself in the silvered mirror was one calculated to shrivel the stoutest heart. Half-an-hour's journey away was the moon upon which we were hastening in a mad descent. Should we reach her surface, the impact would be sufficient to smash our machine into splinters, and ourselves into a shapeless mass. In that agonising moment it seemed all was lost. Bitterly I cursed the folly of our lack of perception. With shame I confess I lost control of my senses. If salvation had been left to my sagacity, disaster would have been the result.

And then Sandy proved the wisdom of our choice when we elected him to lead us. In a moment or two I heard his voice, soft in his kindly remonstrance.

"Come, come, Jim old fellow, you must not rave like that. Pull yourself together, man! It was a trying moment, I'll grant. But we're out of the danger now."

I woke to the realisation we were once more upon an even keel. Paul stood beside me, white and shaken. And Sandy – God bless him for his nobility of mind – turned himself about that he should not see the look of shame upon my face.

"I'm sorry, Sandy, for my foolish weakness," I said huskily, "I promise, honestly, it shall not happen again. I thought myself stronger to face an emergency, but... well, I'm thoroughly ashamed."

"Say no more, old chap," answered Sandy, kindly. "We are safely through. Let us forget our momentary danger."

"Jim," said Paul quietly, "you need not take all the blame for this weakness. I confess that when I found the machine cant downwards, I was also in a funk. I felt the sweat ooze out of my pores. I did not actually divine the cause, but a thought flashed through my mind it was due to the moon's influence. How on Earth did you bring us out of it, Sandy? It must have been a devilishly quick action."

"Yes, I expect it was," answered Sandy. "And it had to be. Another few moments would have put "paid" to our enterprise.

"When I heard your cry I was bewildered for a second. A quick glance in the mirror revealed the cause of the trouble. We were pulled by the gravitational influence of the moon, which deflected the machine downwards.

"I'm afraid I cannot take the real credit for what was done, because I acted upon instinct rather than judgement. I mean I had no time to weigh the result of my action, and therefore what I did was purely mechanical. Now that I have had time to reason out the plan of sequence, I see exactly what happened.

"I reversed the poles of the aft control which changed repulsion into attraction. The change of power produced a "pull" from the Earth instead of a "push". At the same time, I brought the forward control to zero. With the power reversed aft and the forward power out, the prow of the machine shot upwards. Immediately I brought the forward control to full velocity ahead, and at the same time changed back the aft control to detraction.

"If," concluded Sandy with a smile, "I may use a vulgarism here, we shot past the moon like greased lightning – and we're safe again. That's all boys."

Sandy told his story very modestly. Nevertheless, both Paul and I realised in our hearts his action had been heroic. Thank God there came a time when I was able to look my comrade in the face, knowing I had won back my honour.

Chapter 6

Some little time after the exciting incident recorded in the last chapter, we reverted to the subject again. We did so, for one thing, because of a desire to stimulate our minds in the necessity of weighing more carefully the probabilities of the future. There was also another reason, and this is of equal importance.

We had now been on the voyage for eight terrestrial days. Every moment of that period, except the hours of sleep, had been full of interest. A unique voyage like ours was well calculated to grip the interest. Ahead of us, however, was a journey which would extend over a period of nearly ten months.

Unique as the voyage was, we saw that the continuous sameness would soon pall, and ultimately drive us nearly mad. We therefore decided to institute a programme of alternate education (in the form of talks on various subjects), and relaxation (in the form of music, etc). I am convinced it was a wise procedure, for there is nothing so calculated to dwarf the intellect as mental inactivity. Let me record one or two instances of our talks and of our relaxations.

As I intimated a moment ago, we first reverted to the circumstances which nearly brought an untimely end to our adventures.

"I must candidly admit," began Sandy, "I eliminated all ideas of the proximity of the moon. We all knew the moon was new at the commencement of the voyage, but believing also that Venus would 'drag' the machine in an opposite direction to that in which our satellite moved, I felt certain we should be free of her influence."

"Speaking for myself," observed Paul, "I did not consider the question at all. After the machine was completed and we were ready to begin the flight, it was Venus only I saw – the goal of our ambition – and not impediments in the way."

"I'm afraid it was the same with me, Paul," said I. "If the magnetic antennae gripped Venus, as we anticipated it would, and as we subsequently found it did, then I'll tell you what I saw. It was the supremacy of the human scientific mind, working along orthodox lines, and making the "impossible" possible. That, and a clear, unobstructed journey to Venus. I see now my attitude may be construed into the worst of all human failings – that of a blind, don't-care-a-damn for probabilities optimism."

"Yes," answered Sandy, quietly. "I have thought often that this very human failing was one of the principle contributory causes which lost the 'Titanic'. As you very aptly put it, Jim: 'The supremacy of the human scientific mind, making the impossible possible.' Then, through a lack of proper discernment of values – disaster. Over-confidence in one's ability or underestimation of some small detail – that is the trouble in most cases where things have gone wrong.

"Much as we have been able to achieve; far outdistancing the most modern of scientific experts, yet the lesson we have been taught should bring home to us our limitations, and make us humble. If we view the matter in its true perspective, and we are honest with ourselves, we see that we were entirely at fault. We should have foreseen that the proximity of the moon to our course was a factor of the greatest importance."

"By the way," interposed Paul. "Did either of you form an idea where we should have crashed? Of course I was boxed up in the fore-cabin so had no opportunity of seeing anything in the mirror."

"Good heavens! Paul, no!" I exclaimed. "One hasty glance I gave and that was sufficient. My mind was paralysed with the shock. Everything became blurred, consequently I had no visualised impression."

"It is not strange how varied are the effects of shock upon the brain," said Sandy, musingly. "Of course we know generally, and you, Paul, through your medical studies, know particularly that every member of the body functions from the brain. Sometimes, under shock, the vision is blurred, at other times clarified. Speech at times becomes inarticulate, at other times voluble. The limbs, too, are affected in the same contrariwise way. Sometimes with the awful numbness of paralysis, at other times with surprising agility.

"Shock affected you and I in different ways, Jim. Not that I wish to recall a painful episode, old man. I merely speak of cause and effect. A common cause but opposite effects.

"Don't look crestfallen, man," noticing, I suppose, my shamed countenance. "The time will come when we shall probably have to change places. No! As I said a moment ago, a common cause, but opposite effects. You say, Jim, your vision was blurred. Well, mine became clarified, and while my limbs worked with lightning-like (though mechanical) precision, my brain, through the organ of sight, received such an impression that I can see it yet. In fact, I think I could sketch with fair accuracy the details of the lunar surface upon which we should have crashed. I have very little doubt it would have been in the region of the 'Mare Crisium.'"

"The lunar day had just commenced, had it not?" queried Paul. "I wonder if the Lunarians saw our machine?"

"I scarcely think so," replied Sandy. "From what the chief intimated in his log, I fancy the Lunarians keep more to the vicinity of the ringed volcanoes. It is there the huge doors are fixed leading to their subterranean towns. But to come down to the commonplace, how about dinner, boys?"

Perhaps our method and menu will interest, probably amuse, the reader.

Seeing that our foods and drinks were in tabloid form, there was no real need of following the usual domestic order. Yet for the sake of association we followed it. That is to say, we laid the cloth upon the chart room table, and placed thereon three small dishes. In each was an assortment of tabloids which gave us all the satisfaction associated with a five-course dinner of approved style. We knew the composition of each tabloid by its colour. Oxtail soup tabloids were yellow, chicken tabloids white, concentrated beef red, and vegetable tabloids greenish-brown. The fruit tabloids were orange in tone. As our teeth were not brought into use for mastication, we kept them in order and firmness by chewing a small portion of red rubber for half-an-hour, three times a day.

Our ordinary drinks were solidified tabloids, which dissolved when placed in the mouth, and entirely satisfied our thirst. We also had a case of brandy on board. This, I need scarcely say, was purely for medicinal purposes.

And so the days passed pleasantly along. We found no difficulty in picking up messages and musical programmes, transmitted from every source upon the Earth. Also, we had made several attempts at tuning in to Venus, but with negative results. We did not despair, however. We believed some results would obtain as we approached nearer the planet.

There was one feature of our hours of relaxation I enjoyed to the full. That was Paul's singing, Sandy being the accompanist with his guitar. Paul had an exquisite tenor voice, rich in quality and strikingly pure in tone. He had the confidence of a master who feared no criticism. He never "sought" for a note, but was bold in attack and polished in execution.

One day he sang with delightful expression a song with a theme as old as the race – a love song. As he sang, one could easily visualise the man, with pulse a-throb with the intensity of his joy, protesting his love. The girl, adorable in her hesitancy, eventually thrilling to his embrace.

"Yes," said I, when Paul had concluded his song, "you sing it beautifully, old man, and the theme is ever new."

"O, I don't know," said Paul carelessly. "The theme may be ever new Jim, but I sing that song merely because its range is within my scope – not because I have any intrinsic sympathy with the theme. Personally I sometimes wonder whether there is such a commodity as real love.

"One sees evidence of a momentary glamour; a physical fascination, which time dispels. But the theme of the novelists – the self-sacrificing Love seems non-existent. At least..."

"Paul!" interrupted Sandy. "You are cynical. Let me tell you of an incident which is true and came under my own observation."

Chapter 7

Sandy first saw that everything was in order about the machine, then proceeded to narrate the "Real Love" incident that had come under his observation. As he took his seat, I noticed his shoulders stiffen as though he would prepare himself to meet a blow. I did not know then what the telling of the story would cost him.

"It is just a simple story," began Sandy "yet one of a Love that expected nothing in return – nothing but the Joy and Happiness of the one loved. The point I wish to emphasise is that the man found his supreme joy just in loving. I shall call the man by an assumed name. Here is the story:

"John Dalton stood by the low wall that separated his beautifully laid-out gardens from the road. Since he had come into his possessions through the death of an uncle, it had been his daily custom of rising early, partaking of a light breakfast, and then, until an hour before lunch, working hard upon a book he was writing. He lunched at noon, and from 11am until noon he enjoyed a slow meditative perambulation of his gardens. The sweet-scented flowers, the soft carpet of grass, the tree, the birds, all refreshed and reinvigorated him, and fitted him for the renewed labours of the afternoon.

"He had taken his turn of the gardens and was about to retrace his steps when, from the other side of the wall, a voice arrested him. He stood a moment in silence.

"'Now, Sis,' said a boyish voice, 'there's nobody about, so you can tell me now, can't you?'

"'But you would not understand, Jimmy – you are only a child.'

"John Dalton knew the voice to be feminine, a voice full of exquisite sweetness.

"'Darn,' he said indignantly, 'a child indeed, and me twelve years old? What about yourself, you're only eighteen. But never mind, Sis, I didn't mean to hurt you. You just tell me.'

"'Well, Jimmy,' replied the girlish voice, so beautifully modulated, and yet the listener could detect a note of pain and of tiredness therein. 'It's like this. When I was a little girl my illness did not seem to matter very much, but since I have got bigger and older, I have wanted something that other girls have. Dad and Mum and you, Jimmy, dear, are all so good to me. But, Jimmy. I want a sweetheart!'

"Evidently, a bomb had burst. There was silence for a moment, and then a gasp. 'Gosh, Sis! I didn't know it was this that was worrying you. And as you know, no chap would like a... No! No! Don't cry, Sis, dear. Don't cry! Only I don't know what to say.'"

"And the silent listener knew that the boy's eyes were tear-filled as he strove to comfort his sister.

"Cautiously making his way to the low wall, John Dalton, with a smile of sympathetic tolerance, took a peep to see who these young folk were. The sight he saw moved his big heart with compassion.

"Lying prone in a spinal carriage was a young girl, her face turned towards the brother, who had brought her out for her daily airing. Slowly she turned her face, and when Dalton saw it, he started in wondering astonishment. Nature's compensation had been at work.

The poor body was weak and misshapen, but the face was ethereal in its beauty. No woman had ever stirred his pulse as yet, or caused his heart to beat quicker than the normal. But now, as he turned away, vague disturbances seemed to take place in his mind. He smiled to himself and called himself every sort of fool. Nevertheless, that afternoon, not one word was added to the story he was writing.

"Careful enquiry among his servants elicited the who and the where of these young folk, and the following afternoon saw Dalton, with a choice bunch of flowers, on his way to her home.

"'I am informed you have an invalid daughter,' said Dalton to her mother by way of apology for his visit. 'I have ventured to bring her a few flowers.' And the smile that lit up the girl's face when he saw her was ample reward for his gift.

"'Yes,' she said in answer to his query. 'I love flowers, Mr Dalton. Their beautiful fragrance helps me wonderfully on my bad days. Yet it seems so cruel to cut them. I wish I could walk amongst them, then I should be so happy. But you see I have... I have to lay here.'

"From once a week his visits became twice and then three times a week. And then every afternoon found him by her side (to the detriment of his book, may it be said). But John Dalton had found something that transcended even the success of his literary efforts. He had found Love!

"Often now her young brother would bring her up to Dalton's house on sunny days, and there upon the velvety lawn he would sit beside her carriage and tell her of his struggles as a journalist before he came into his possessions.

"One day as he sat by her carriage, he noticed a peculiarly pensive look upon her face. It was as though she debated some complex problem.

"'What is troubling you, Princess? he whispered. 'Are you not happy?'

"'Happy?' said she tremulously. 'Why, Mr Dalton, I am so happy that sometimes I forget I am not like other girls. But how can I ever repay you for all your kindness? That is what troubles me at times.'

"'That is nonsense!' he cried brusquely. And then gently he said, 'but you are like other girls. You have a warm heart and a beautiful spirit – and Princess, you can repay me. Yes, you can. I want you for my sweetheart – my wife!'

"'But you cannot! You must not!' she cried wildly. 'Mr Dalton, you know it is impossible!'

"'In the first place, "Mr Dalton" be hanged!' he retorted, whilst simultaneously taking possession of her two hands upon the coverlet. 'My name is John. Listen, dearest. When I was at Cambridge I met a young Hindoo, and though there was a difference of race and colour between us, we became fast friends. He had a sister whom he loved passionately. And, rare as it is among Hindoo women, she was suffering like you. So passionately did he love his sister that he told me he intended devoting his life to a study of this complaint. He questioned if there was a cure, but he hoped to discover something that, at least, would ameliorate somewhat his sister's suffering and helplessness.

"His success has been greater than his wildest dream – his sister is cured. I have written to him about you. The reply came this morning. You are going to marry me, Princess, and I am going to take you to India. I have faith to believe he can help you. However, cure or no cure, you are going to be mine. Mine! Darling! Until death us do part!"

Sandy paused in his recital. Both Paul and I had been absorbed in the story. The sudden break seemed to jar upon Paul, who, at times, proved his nationality by his impetuosity.

"Yes, yes, Sandy!" he cried impatiently. "But what was the sequel?"

"The sequel was good," said Sandy quietly, controlling himself with an effort.

"Two years passed, and Jimmy, now a sturdy lad of 14, waited at the Indian docks for the arrival of the Indian liner 'Carfax'. Wild with excitement he saw the 'Carfax' berthed, and the passengers began to come ashore. With quick perception he saw his brother-in-law. But who was the wonderful creature by his side? He was not left long in doubt. Before his brother-in-law could grasp his hand, the "wonderful creature", walking with the grace of a young queen, had thrown her arms around his neck. 'Jimmy!' she said, between laughter and tears. 'Jimmy! Don't you know your own Sis? Is it not just too wonderful for words?'

"And Jimmy was not ashamed of the tears that coursed down his cheeks as he locked his young arms about her and kissed her. As she said, 'It was just too wonderful for words.'

"That is the story, boys." concluded Sandy, "and I recommend its application to you, Paul, as a wholesome purge. Don't grow cynical, old man. That story is true!"

With a queer slope of the shoulders, Sandy left us, and went into the fore cabin, closing the door behind him.

"Jim," whispered Paul, somewhat startled. "That story is bound up intimately with old Sandy. Did you notice how difficult the last part was to tell us. I wonder if..."

"No, no Paul!" I answered hastily. "Sandy would not like us to pry. Let us..."

Unperceived by us, Sandy had returned to the cabin. "It's all right, boys. She was my wife – the sweetest creature God ever let a man have. Three glorious years I had with her, then a terrible railway accident claimed her as a victim. That is why I have since been a wanderer."

Chapter 8

There is one other of our conversations I wish to record. I record it because, strangely enough, it had a distinct bearing upon our subsequent discoveries. I should not impose this conversation upon the reader – feeling, as I do, that the reader is more concerned with our actual adventures upon Venus – but for the fact of coincidence. Sandy's story, recorded in the last chapter, and this conversation, were both attended by a most remarkable sequel.

We were somewhat at a loose end for some fresh diversion when Sandy introduced a subject with uncharacteristic suddenness.

"Man!" said Sandy, crisply. "His origin, development and destiny. What are your opinions relative to this subject, boys? Paul, you old materialist, what have you to say?"

Paul's face lit up with one of his rare smiles. "Yes, Sandy, I suppose I am a materialist," he answered. "The subject is a rather wide one, but if I may put my opinions or beliefs in a few brief sentences, they are these.

"I believe that the most advanced vertebrate, man, was evolved primarily from a lowly unicellular organism. From thence he passed by stages, through millions of years, to worm, fish, reptile, mammal, until he has reached what he is to-day. In very truth, he is of the earth, earthly. Man is still developing or evolving towards a higher state of existence. What that higher state may be I cannot pretend to suggest. That, briefly, is my belief, relative to the race. As regards man as an individual, each adds his quota to the sum total of human development, after which, his work being completed, he dies and is committed to the grave. That is his destiny – the grave. The destiny of every human organism upon Earth." And Paul concluded with dogmatic finality.

I loved Paul, but I listened to the recital of his horribly materialistic creed with rising anger. "'Lowly origin?' 'Development through reptile and mammal?' 'Destiny – the grave?' Rubbish!

"I do not believe your statements of creed, Paul," said I, hotly. "They are contrary to ascertained facts. Man was a definite and separate act of creation. He fell from his first estate and his development has been a moral development ever ascending to his original purity. Not only so, but what of his soul?"

"Very well, Jim," answered Paul, smilingly, and for the first time I found Paul's smile to be irritating. "Let us consider your question first. Tell me what you mean by 'the soul'."

"I mean that part of our nature which, by universal instinct, desire and consent, lives on after physical death," I replied shortly.

"Then the soul, as you conceive it, is non-existent, Jim," said Paul with conviction. "Every department of the entire person, whether moral, mental or physical, functions by the brain. Paralyse the brain and every function ceases. There is no difference between a man who is an imbecile and yourself, Jim, save in one respect. You can think beautiful thoughts; aspire to noble living and heroic actions, while he grovels in mud and filth. Your beautiful thoughts and noble aspirations have a material origin – the brain. The imbecile grovels brutish and bestial through lack of brain. The only difference between you is a few ounces of grey matter – and matter is material, therefore perishable. Perhaps it would be better to say that in one case the brain functions, in the other the brain is functionless.

"No, old fellow, man does not survive physical death. It is the universal fear of death that has produced universal desire and consent for immortality. And fear and desire are both the product of the brain."

"But surely you believe in a God?" I queried, with spirit. "You surely are not ass enough to believe that no controlling mind is behind all causation? And if there is a Personal Being who plans and controls, surely He has something better for His highest creation than oblivion?"

"You fly off at a tangent, Jim," replied Paul, quietly. "That some controlling force is at the back of nature only a fool would deny. But whether that force may be termed personal or impersonal is too big a subject for me. Assuming your hypothesis is correct – that a personal intelligent Being is at the back of all things, that neither proves nor disproves a continuity of life for man. I am afraid you are right up in the air, old chap, while I can be in one place only. Like dear old Jack London's character, 'Ernest Everhand', my feet are on the earth, solid and stolid and safe."

I am afraid I was never good at intensive debate. While I had inward convictions which completely denied Paul's sweeping assertions, I could not assemble them in coherent order or force. I very lamely fell back upon the usual formula given under such circumstances, and petulantly told Paul I did not believe his aspect of the case.

"Prove me wrong, old boy!" said Paul with good-humoured banter.

"No," said Sandy quietly before I could reply, "Jim would have a difficulty in proving you wrong, Paul, because his methods are wrong. Jim, we are now well-seasoned friends, you, Paul and I, and you will not take amiss at what I say. Heat gets a fellow nowhere, except it be in a quicksand. He is soon overwhelmed and lost. Paul is convincing because he can assemble his thoughts with coolness, with logic and with precision. Many an indifferent cause has been won by Paul's method, and many a good cause has been lost by your method, Jim.

"But though Paul is convincing, it does not necessarily follow that his deductions are true. That would be a fatal mistake to make. Truth is immutable. It cannot change. Beliefs change, opinions change, convictions change – truth, never. So what we have to decide is, what is true in regard to man's destiny. His origin and development are both intimately bound up with his destiny, but as we are not debating in public, we need not be fastidious. Let it be his destiny. The grave and oblivion, or continuity of existence?

"Paul, old man, I can well understand your attitude. You have always studied along materialistic lines. Matter sits rigidly at the base of your thinking, and therefore you see nothing but a physical basis for life in all its varied activities. Even in death you see the same basic principle, for death to you is release back to the primal constituent elements.

"With a part of your reasoning I am in accord. With you, I believe that man is an evolved being; that he has developed to the position he holds to-day among the galaxy of animated life. But we part company at your gloomy terminus. You halt humanity at the grave. I say with equal conviction that there is no halt. Not even a 'marking time,' but a continuation of the march. I will...

"Mere sentiment, Sandy!" interposed Paul. "Sentiment! If not, then tabulate your proofs!"

"No, Paul, I am unable to furnish you with proofs, because proof in this matter is one of sympathetic perception. That is to say: the sunset has no charm for one who is blind, and music is meaningless to one who is deaf. In the same sense, immateriality is unappreciable and unknown to a materialist.

"You intimated that the fear of death was responsible for the universal consent and desire for immortality. I do not think so. I believe there are thousands of human beings who, having been taught that wrongdoing must be severely punished, would gladly believe in oblivion at death, but they cannot so believe. To believe so they would have to violate their own deep-seated convictions.

"It is true I cannot give you proof, if by proof you mean an absolute demonstration, but to me and to all who have sympathetic perception the higher capabilities of man, such as honour, love, duty, faith, etc, speak of an alliance to something outside the materialistic basis of matter.

"Perhaps in my case it is this very belief – a belief that held me and still holds me with a tenacious grip – that kept me sane when I saw my darling crushed and mangled in the train disaster. I shall see her again, Paul! I do not know where. But just as I see you and Jim sitting here with me; just as I talk to you here, so I am convinced I shall see her again and talk with her."

"Well, old chap, while I am satisfied with my view of things," said Paul, soberly, "I'll say nothing further to contradict that wonderful belief of yours. Still, I'll shake old Jim by the hand, because a moment or so ago I thought he'd like to murder me!"

Of course there was no anger in my heart for dear old Paul, and I shook him by the hand, apologising for my foolish conduct in the debate. But if only the three of us could have known the discoveries ahead of us, there would have been no debate. Just an awesome wonder!

Chapter 9

It seemed that the fates decreed we were not to reach our destination without further adventure. We [subsequently] passed through two experiences of a rather terrifying nature; [one of utter despair]; the other, equally startling, rendered us mystified and perplexed. The first occurred on my watch, and had we been but a little farther advanced upon our journey, no power could have averted a terrible catastrophe. A former experience had taught us that forethought and vigilance were of the utmost importance, and I can say with confidence there was not a moment of the journey but where a faithful look-out was maintained.

I have no wish to vaunt myself, but both Sandy and Paul will agree I was the keenest observer astronomically. It was my supreme delight when upon watch to observe the starry heavens, especially the displacement of the planets among the stars. Neptune, Uranus and Saturn were, of course, too far away to give me unrest, but I had no difficulty in seeing Jupiter and Mars.

Our old world still continued to be the brightest star in the heavens, and when her sky was devoid of clouds I could see her continental areas. And what to me was more significant, I could detect the glint of the sun as it was reflected from terrestrial waters. Venus was growing rapidly in bulk, but even yet was too far away for me to [have any settled convictions relating] to her axial rotations, or whether her atmosphere approximated to that of the Earth. I also saw the planet Mercury to much better advantage than ever before.

On one of my watches I had been interested in observing Mercury and his position relative to an adjacent point of light. Observing the planet some hours later, I found the distance between the two had considerably widened – and in a direction contrary to what I considered it should. Thinking quite naturally that the point of light had been a fixed star, I was greatly exercised in my mind at this discovery. It meant that if my observations were correct, Mercury was moving in a direction opposite to the rest of the planetary hosts. Now I knew of no logical reason why such should be the case. It was contrary to all planetary motion.

Observing Mercury some time later, I saw how easily I had been deceived. That which I had taken to be a fixed point of light was itself moving, and moving with incredible swiftness. Its position among the stars was changing every moment.

I logged my observations, and Sandy, looking through and checking the log of each watch, commented upon its entry.

"What do you make of this discovery of yours, Jim?" asked Sandy.

"I scarcely know what to think," I replied, hesitatingly. "Finding my first assumption wrong, I naturally studied the little body with greater interest and care. I then supposed it to be the hypothetical planet of Romance – "Vulcan", which, as you know, is believed to circle inside the orbit of Mercury. But again

I found my assumption wrong. Now I'm completely fogged. But come both of you and look for yourselves; perhaps one of you may be able to offer some logical explanation."

A great surprise awaited us. That moving point of light had vanished from sight as completely as though it had never been.

"It's vanished!" I exclaimed, with extreme vexation. "If that don't beat the band. I saw..."

"Your grandmother's nightlight," murmured Paul with a chuckle. "And now some busybody's been and snuffed it."

"No, Paul. I'll not be jested out of it," I answered Paul's banter. "I saw it distinctly, and watched for hours its race apparently upon a definite orbit. But it's not there now, and that is equally certain."

"Of course we believe you old chap!" said Paul. "But its disappearance is very mysterious indeed. What d'you think of it, Sandy?"

"It is rather difficult to form an opinion," replied Sandy with something of anxiety in his tone. "You are the only one who has observed it, Jim. Are you sure it could not have been Vulcan? Vulcan, if existing, would be very much smaller than Mercury, and the immense distance would render its size very small indeed. I mean, do you think you could have been mistaken?"

"No," I replied. "I am very certain it could not have been Vulcan. I am convinced it moved outside the orbit of Mercury. In fact, I am almost convinced it moved outside the orbit of Venus. It is dreadfully vexing to think we have lost it. It was quite an interesting little body to observe."

My turn of duty came round again, with no fresh light upon the vexed question of the little body's disappearance. Paul and Sandy had each watched in turn, but with negative results. As I went towards the silvered mirror, a thought flashed into my mind with startling suddenness. I suppose the reason why such a thought had not presented itself before was because of its apparent absurdity. But with my mind rested by sleep, it seemed now all too clear. That light was none other than reflected sunlight from a substance revolving outside the orbit of Venus. And if that was true, we were in a position of positive danger.

"Sandy! Paul!" I cried, in sudden excitement. "I believe I have partially solved the riddle."

And as quickly as possible, I told them my fears. With one bound, Sandy sprang to the forward control, while, just as quickly, Paul rushed to the rear control.

"All right, Jim!" cried Sandy. "While Paul and I watch the control, tell us again your fears. Pray God they will prove groundless."

“Well, boys,” said I, “I believe that the light I saw was really reflected sunlight from a small mass of matter revolving around the Sun, between the orbits of Venus and the Earth. It is probably of cometary origin, detached from the parent mass at some remote epoch by contact with another body, and captured by the Sun’s influence. It’s terrible velocity would prevent it being drawn into the Sun, yet its speed is not too high to further disintegrate its mass. At the same time...”

“Do you think, Jim, it may be the remains of a moon of the Venus system?” queried Paul.

“No, Paul, I do not,” I answered. “I feel certain it is Solar and not planetary influence holding it upon its path. I was going to add that its mass is so insignificant even compared with the asteroids that no terrestrial observer could possibly hope to detect it. I...”

“Look out! Stand by!” cried Sandy, his voice rendered harsh by excitement.

There was little need for his harsh command. Before I could complete my sentence, and even as Sandy spoke, our machine shuddered from stem to stern. We knew at once it was not the shock of collision. Sandy and Paul stood irresolute at the control, Paul waiting for a command, and Sandy fearing to issue one. There was no abatement of speed upon our machine, and still the horrible quivering continued as though our machine would shiver into shreds.

At that moment I caught a glimpse of something that nearly froze the blood in my veins. A huge mass of apparently irregular rock, suffused with a soft glow, was rushing with terrible speed athwart our path. I had no time for fine analysis, but knew at once that the point of light I had lost sight of – as well as this rushing mass – was one and the same.

In the hasty glance I gave to it, I judged it to be about three miles across. It seemed to be charged with some mysterious force which gave to it a softened surface glow, and of such a nature that, instinctively, I knew to be the malignant power affecting our machine. All this I saw and felt in the twinkling of an eye.

I had no opportunity of gathering comfort by looking at my two patient comrades. For now, instead of a hasty glance, my eyes were fixed upon that rushing menace ahead. It fascinated me! It held me in an awful spell! [I could see that its terrible velocity would carry it past us before we reached its path, although at the same time, I feared its close proximity would still be disastrous.]

And then, by supreme effort of will, I broke the spell which held me.

“Get ready to alter the controls when I say, boys!” I cried. “I can see the object now, and it’s rushing right across our path! Now! Now! Reverse the poles, Paul! Quick, for heaven’s sake! Shut off the forward control, Sandy! Good God, man! What...?”

“Can’t!” cried Sandy desperately, “Something’s gone amiss!”

Chapter 10

Since that fateful moment when we nearly crashed upon the moon, I have repeatedly avowed I never wished to live again through such a moment. But I can honestly vouch that when Sandy cried out so despairingly that the forward control was inoperative, I found that to be a more trying moment. In the former experience I completely lost control of my senses; in the latter I was sane, but with a calm despair. In the former I was simply numb; in the latter I felt every moment of it.

And it was horrible in the extreme.

The influence of that rushing mass of matter was magnetic, and afterwards we found its range of influence to be just over 1,000 miles. The effect upon our mechanism was such that the forward control could not be brought to zero. And while we could reverse the poles of the aft battery, instead of the speed becoming less, it accelerated!

As I write this account I live over and over again those fateful moments, and even now the perspiration streams from my pores. The acceleration of speed brought us within an ace of death, and had we been but a few miles further upon our journey nothing could have saved us. A bare six miles separated us when that terrible mass of matter rushed across our bows, and it was by the proverbial hair's breadth that we escaped.

Even as it was, the experience was terrifying in the extreme, for our machine quivered like an aspen leaf for over three-quarters of an hour. Thank God we found, upon examination, that no permanent harm had been done to the machine.

Before leaving this incident I may say that both Sandy and Paul thought my supposition to be the correct one – that this floating mass of matter was really a fragment of a comet smashed by contact with another body, æons before, while probably in a plastic state, and captured by the Sun. Having come under the Sun's influence, it will probably continue in its orbit until the final disruption of the solar system. We prayed this would be the only one of its kind upon our journey, and our prayer was answered.

Now let me record the other incident. One which left us mystified and perplexed.

It was Paul's spell of observational duty. I was busy preparing for dinner, and Sandy had tuned in to the Earth in order to pick up current topics. After a while he intimated his desire to switch the wireless director on to Venus.

[None of us] could exactly say what we hoped for, except that should there be sentient life upon Venus, and should they be skilled in wireless, we thought something might happen to reveal their presence. We realised all the difficulties facing us. We felt it to be almost too remote for possibility that any semblance of coincidence should be found between our codes.

But we felt that should our attempt interfere with their instruments then they in turn would attempt an investigation of its meaning and send out some kind of response. We concluded quite reasonably that their response would be as unintelligible to us as ours would be to them. Still, as I said a moment ago, we hoped that something would occur which would indicate the presence of intelligent beings.

It was the simplest of experiments that Sandy tried. He first took the dead focus of Venus from the silvered mirror, then set the direction true upon that line. (I have already indicated that the work of the special director was to localise the path of etheric disturbance). We knew, of course, the distance Venus was ahead of us, seeing that we took dead reckoning every eight hours.

Gradually, Sandy extended the wavelength until the indicator recorded the distance required. He then tried a simple interference. Three dots, two dashes, a pause. Three dots, two dashes, a pause – and so he continued for a quarter-of-an-hour. For a further quarter-of-an-hour he rested quietly with the 'phones on. Thereafter he continued almost without pause for eight hours.

"It is of little use, Jim," said he, finally. "Whether there are folk on Venus or not must remain an unsettled problem for now. I expect we shall have to possess our souls in patience until we arrive there."

"Yes," I answered. "I expect it is rather on the foolish side to expect an answer to our call. The manner of communication will undoubtedly be vastly different from ours. Our articulation is..."

"Hist!" exclaimed Paul, with startling suddenness. "What's that?!"

Paul's sudden ejaculation pulled Sandy and I up short, and we listened with bated breath. "Tic, tic, tic- ti-c, ti-c" – then a pause. Instinctively we turned to the clock dial of our indicator. With fast-beating hearts we stood fearing to put on the 'phones. We saw the tiny needle tap the stud, and we heard the faint metallic "tic" of contact. "Tic, tic, tic- ti-c, ti-c" – and again a pause.

"For the love of heaven, boys, put on the 'phones!" cried Sandy in his excitement. "It is an answer to our call!" And immediately we all three donned the headphones.

Clear as a bell there came the musical replica of our own call. Yet such is the perversity of human intelligence under stress of excitement. Though we knew it to be an answer, and were quite certain that our director precluded the possibility of Earth disturbance, we could not satisfy ourselves that the answer came from Venus. As though the same thought occurred to each simultaneously, we discarded the 'phones and looked blankly at one another.

"Is it, boys?" queried Paul huskily. "Is it really... an answer? Or is there any possibility of monkeying?"

Our gaze turned again to the indicator. The needle was still tap-tapping its message. Scarcely knowing what I was doing, I switched off the indicator and turned it towards the Earth. Instantly the tapping ceased.

"It is a message – an answer to our call," said Sandy in an awesome whisper. "It is sent from Venus. Our call reached their instruments, and though they did not understand its real importance, they have responded in like manner. To think we should be the first in the history of the universe to establish the fact of life on other planets! I am convinced it is a true discovery. True as the fact of our own existence!"

After a while we were more composed, and with the abatement of excitement there came a moment of doubt. Paul was by nature extremely cautious in accepting new ideas. He had to see a thing error-proof before he gave intellectual assent. It was he who voiced the doubt.

"I am not at all certain we have discovered evidence of intelligent life upon Venus, Sandy," said he. "Is there not a possibility that some peculiar physical condition caused the apparent response? Would it be feasible to suggest the possibility of an ætheric recoil, similar to the atmospheric rebound which we know as an echo?

"We know that our director limits the area of disturbance to a very narrow diameter. We also know from the indicator the wavelength equalled the distance of Venus. Is it then not more sane to believe that the disturbance caused by our call touched some part of the planet and set up a reaction or a recoil of corresponding force and power? The disturbance would then return exactly as sent out."

"I am not sure, but there may well be truth in your suggestion, Paul," replied Sandy, somewhat crestfallen. ["I was so absorbed in sending out the call that I did not allow sufficient time to elapse between the transmissions – hence this possible recoil wasn't detected sooner. It was only after I went off air that the apparent answer came.] And, as you suggest, it may simply be the recoil of ætheric disturbance. Switch the director on to Venus again, Jim, and see if we can solve the problem.

I did as Sandy wished. As soon as the director faced the true direction of Venus there came again, in perfect rhythmic spacing, the exact call we sent out. We left the director in the same position, and the remarkable thing was the tapping continued for exactly the same period as Sandy had taken in sending it out. It then suddenly ceased.

It seemed very disappointing to believe that some physical cause lay at the root of our apparent success. But if we had known the real solution our disappointment would have been instantly turned into joy. We were shortly to know this.

Chapter 11

It seemed very disappointing to believe that ætheric recoil lay at the root of our apparent success. Sandy took the disappointment rather badly for his usually optimistic nature. In fact, for a time he was very unlike his real self. We knew from the commencement of our voyage that disappointment and disillusionment would play a prominent part in our enterprise. It could not be otherwise in such an adventure as that upon which we were now engaged. And Sandy was as conscious of this as either Paul or I.

It was very gratifying to us, therefore, when we saw signs that our comrade and chief was taking a more sane view of things, and soon he was his old self again.

"You stated the case against so lucidly, Paul, that I'm afraid I resented your logic," said Sandy, with a half apologetic air. "I felt so certain that at last we had established the fact of intelligent life upon Venus, that..."

"And so we may have established that fact," interposed Paul with a smile. "I only stated the case against in order that we may not jump to conclusions before we had anything like incontrovertible proof.

"The apparent answer to our call may be genuine enough; but, I want to know this beyond reasonable doubt before I start to believe there's intelligent life out there. Even if the apparent answer turns out to be the effect of ætheric recoil – then that neither proves nor disproves the existence or non-existence of life upon Venus.

"It may be the case that we are unable to find a definitive answer to this vexed question until we reach our destination. Assuming we reach Venus in safety, we shall know then one way or the other with a certainty which cannot be denied. My advice, then, is to let things remain as they are until we alight upon the planet."

Sandy requested me to log our distance from Venus. Upon complying I found it to be just over one million miles. By simple calculation I found that a message sent out would take about six seconds upon the journey. So that if Paul's theory of ætheric recoil was correct, our instrument would be affected in about thirteen seconds.

Sandy then sent out the simple call he had first instituted – three dots, two dashes. I counted off the seconds, but no answering disturbance touched our indicator. He waited ten minutes, and again sent out the call – with the same negative result.

"That seems to disprove my theory of ætheric recoil, at any rate," observed Paul quietly. "Try once more Sandy, and see. Good heavens... Look!" And Paul pointed to the indicator.

There was little need for Paul's request to look, for all three of us not only saw the needle move, but heard its metallic contact upon the stud. The time had long since passed to connect the present disturbance with the call sent out. Not only so, but a further proof that the recoil theory was untenable lay in the fact that the disturbance continued. We each donned the headphones and again, clear as a bell, came the musical answer to our call – three short notes and two of longer duration.

"What a fool I am!" cried Sandy, suddenly. "Connect up the microphone, Jim, and switch on the loudspeaker. We will try another method. I wonder why no one thought of it before. I'll..."

"But that will be of no use, man!" Paul remonstrated, divining what Sandy was about to attempt. "Even if it is someone upon Venus answering our call, they are merely duplicating our message. They cannot possibly understand its purport. How much less, then, will they understand speech, whether English, French, or any other terrestrial language? Still, I am sorry, old man. Of course, you are the boss. I'm afraid I was rather impetuous."

"It's quite all right, Paul," answered Sandy with a laugh. "Of course you are impetuous. Is that not one of your fundamental characteristics? Nevertheless, old impetuous, I'm not going to listen to arguments against this time. I am going to make the attempt. And if English and French happens to be unsuccessful, then I'll try good broad Scotch."

Sandy stood in front of the microphone and with resonant voice said, "Hello! Hello! Can you hear my voice?"

While Sandy took the position with every degree of composure and gravity, I could see upon Paul's face an expression which indicated suppressed mirth. I must confess that I, too, felt somewhat in the same humour, seeing the seeming absurdity of the whole process.

I felt that Paul's reasoning was correct. It was utterly unthinkable to suppose that, even if there were sentient beings upon Venus, their mode of expression would be similar to ours. But in a moment our suppressed hilarity was transformed into amazement, for clear and distinct there came an English word – "Wait!"

A profound silence ensued. Then... "Sandy, old man," said Paul soberly. "This has got me guessing. I heard that word, and it came apparently from the loudspeaker. Of its source, I have no knowledge unless... you can perform ventriloquial tricks, Jim?"

"Whether I have that gift or not, Paul, you know very well I was not responsible for that word," I replied. "And neither was Sandy. It came from a source outside the machine, of that I think we may be satisfied. But from what source leaves me guessing, too."

"It is possible that our director is faulty, and we have picked up one stray word from the Earth," suggested (rather than queried) Paul. "It is the fact of an English word being used that is so puzzling."

"No, Paul," replied Sandy quietly and with perfect composure. "We may preclude the possibility that our director is faulty, also that the word is picked up from any terrestrial source. That word came from Venus!

"I went off the deep end at your logic a short time ago, but with conviction flooding in upon me now, excitement, resentment and unbelief are absent from my being. Yet, certain as I am that word came from Venus, I should be little short of an ass were I to say I can explain the phenomenon of an English word being used. That is altogether beyond me."

"Yes, but good heavens, Sandy! Don't you see what it means? It is not only that an English word was used, but it also means that your call was understood and appreciated. That is, of course, if it did actually come from Venus. Of that I am still in doubt."

Thus Paul fought every inch of the way in his endeavour for conviction. The proof would have to be unimpeachable for him. As for myself, I scarcely knew what to think. And yet it should have been clear both to Paul and myself. We both knew that with the director in true alignment with Venus, it was impossible to pick up any message from Earth. But my thoughts were at that moment interrupted by seeing Sandy take up his position again by the microphone.

"Here goes for an attempt to quash your doubts, old son," said Sandy to Paul. Then, turning to the microphone, he said, slowly and distinctly: "Hello! Hello! We are approaching the globe second in order of distance from the great luminary known as the Sun. We call the globe to which we are fast approaching, 'Venus'. Can you hear me? Do you understand what I have just said?"

Breathlessly we waited to hear the effect of Sandy's message. It came in concise phrasing, and with an exquisite intonation.

"We have known of your coming for many days," said the voice. "Make no conjectures of what you will see and hear when you arrive. No thought you may conceive will fit the revelation awaiting you. Someone has journeyed with you of whom you have no knowledge. From that someone we have had all the information necessary to us of your undertaking. And now for the moment... Farewell!"

Chapter 12

It was a long time before we could make an effort to assimilate the stupendous knowledge given us by the unknown voice. Even when we did settle down to something, mystery still pervaded the whole episode. But of one thing we were now convinced. Even Paul acknowledged his unswerving faith in the fact that the voice came from the planet Venus.

The intriguing mystery was of a two-fold character. How was it possible for beings upon Venus to understand Sandy's question, and answer it in faultless English? And, who was the invisible person who had journeyed, and perhaps even now was travelling with us?

For hours, as we sped on our way, the battle for intellectual assent raged on. One thing was conspicuous by its absence. There was not the slightest suggestion of nervous apprehension upon the part of any of us at the idea of a mysterious and invisible person being on board with us. At last Sandy gave his summing up.

"The whole episode is puzzling in the extreme," said he. "Sometimes I wonder if I am dreaming a wonderful phantasy, with you two as companions to my dream. At other times I realise it is all true. The fact of our overcoming the multitude of obstacles in our way, and of eventually making the journey possible, is wonderful in the extreme.

"Though we should meet now with disaster and death, we should die with the knowledge that no other terrestrial being has achieved what we have achieved. It is marvellous to think that we three are miles ahead of any modern thinker or even dreamer. But of all the wonders we have seen and experienced, this last one is the most inexplicable."

"It's knocked my philosophy into a cocked hat," was Paul's rather inelegant interjection. And though his tone had a tinge of jocularity, it was easily discernible he was deep in an intellectual morass.

“My reason points to the utter foolishness of accepting these things as truth,” he continued thoughtfully. “Yet the facts seem to establish their verity. It seems to me a wearying process in trying to tabulate the pros and cons over again. I feel I must have some sleep.”

“Same here, old fellow,” said Sandy with a smile. “It is my watch, however, so I must keep awake a little longer. But before you lie down, Paul, what do you think of the invisible passenger we are carrying, or supposed to be carrying? I am rather curious to know your opinion, seeing, as you have admitted, you are a pronounced materialist.”

“Honestly, Sandy, old man, I’d rather not discuss it,” replied Paul, rather testily. “Sorry, Sandy, but I feel in a mental maze. As you know, I have been very definite in my opinions – obstinate you will say, old chap – and with the happenings of the past few hours, I feel all at sea. So I’ll say nothing until I have slept upon it.” And with Paul that was final.

“Well,” said I, “I feel too excited to sleep. I’ll take a part of your watch, Sandy, so you and Paul lie down and have a restful nap. I’ll call you in four hours’ time.”

While Sandy and Paul rested, I tried hard to banish from my mind the romantic happenings of the past few hours. I fought against its remembrance in order to attend to things essential and more prosaic. It was necessary now to be extremely careful in logging our position relative to Venus. We were fast approaching the planet, and, of course, the difficulty was we had no data as to the extend of the gravitational pull from Venus. It was very essential that we took dead reckoning.

I found the distance to be 900,000 miles. At 3,500 miles per hour, we should take just over ten days to reach the planet. We could calculate upon another 120 hours of comparative safety. After that, extreme care would have to be exercised. Having proved the distance and logged it, I called Sandy to take his watch.

“You know, Jim, the idea of this mysterious passenger rather fascinates me,” said Sandy, musingly, and I noticed there was a wistful expression upon his face. For the moment I had no thought what was passing through his mind. When the idea did come, it startled me considerably.

“You don’t think...?” I dared not complete that query.

“Yes,” said Sandy, simply. “I’m just wondering, old chap, if it’s... *her*?”

“Sandy!” Paul had awakened and heard the quiet, intensitive utterance, so full of pathos and of a hopeless longing. "Sandy! Great heavens! It cannot be. Gee, old man. I'm sorry to damp even your imagined hope, but don't you see how impossible it is?"

And in the intensity of his sympathy, yet withal, filled with doubt, Paul stretched out his hand to grip the hand of his comrade and chief.

"I'm not so sure that it is impossible," I ventured to remark. "And I will tell you why. It occurs to me to tell you of an incident which I can vouch for as truth. It is quite inexplicable to me, yet the facts are just as I relate them.

"There was a time when I was greatly interested in spiritualistic phenomena. I accepted nothing as proved. I was just an investigator.

"During the period of my interest, a meeting was advertised at which a lady was to give the tenets of spiritualistic beliefs, after which she would prove the fact of clairvoyant perception.

"At the meeting I found myself one of an audience of between sixty and seventy, composed of both sexes of adult age. I knew several of the audience, and knew them to be men and women of no mean intelligence.

"I will pass over the first part of the proceedings as being of no interest to us at the moment. Then came the part which proved so inexplicable to me. I may say in passing the lecturer was a complete stranger to the town, this being her first visit. She intimated there were folk present who were invisible to every other person in the room, except herself. She saw them clearly, and would describe them. A generalisation, however, was no concrete proof, therefore she would particularise to a definite individual who was present in the room.

"With dramatic suddenness, the lecturer turned to me where I was sitting, and, pointing to me, asked if I would agree to her describing folk who were standing close to my side. I agreed to her proposition, but laid it down very definitely that the proof would have to be flawless for me to consent to her description. I should agree to no vague description or suggestion. I would have no one imagine there was collusion between lecturer and subject.

"The lecturer smilingly accepted my conditions, saying that the descriptions given would be flawless and convincing. And to my utter amazement it was even as she declared. The descriptions were perfect, and would admit of not the slightest deception.

"Two years previous to this meeting, two cases of malignant illness and subsequent death occurred with which I was intimately acquainted as visitor and friend. One was a girl, 18 years of age, who died with a malady unknown to me, apart from her case. The other was that of a man in late middle life who died with cancer in the throat. The features of both were known to me to the minutest detail. One, the girl, stood by my right shoulder, said the lecturer; the other, the man, stood by my left shoulder.

"As she first described the girl and then the man, I should have been false to the truth had I said I did not recognise them. As clearly as I knew them in life, so mentally I saw them again. Every feature, look and gesture was described, and such was the faithfulness of delineation that I had no hesitation in believing she actually saw them. There can be no other explanation possible." (This is a true experience of the narrator.)

Chapter 13

"And you say that is a true experience, Jim?" queried Sandy, upon the conclusion of my narrative. I could not help but detect a world of longing in his query.

"It is just as I have told you, Sandy," I responded. "I have exaggerated nothing. I have kept nothing back. Every detail I have given you could be vouched for by each member of that audience who followed the demonstration with breathless interest. The descriptions were perfect, and no other explanation can be given, but that what she described she actually saw."

"It just beats the band, old man," said Paul, looking at Sandy. "We commenced our voyage in the hope of discovering something unique. But it seems to me that unique happenings have now become commonplace in our lives. If we stumble across something which should prove normal to our old existence, then we'll tabulate that as unique; for, indeed, the old order has changed with a vengeance. I'm almost persuaded to believe in your yarn, Jim – but not quite."

As Paul said so continuously, it had to be flawless proof before he gave consent. And somewhere Paul still saw flaws, but refused to point them out.

"I am quite convinced of its truth," said Sandy, quietly. "Of course, I quite understand it is a question of clairvoyant perception. And, if it is indeed her, then God grant me the powers of perception. Should that be denied me, I'll try to be content with the thought that she is near me."

"Sandy, old boy," said Paul, with more wistfulness than I had ever known since my acquaintance with him. "I wish I had your faith. It does not seem difficult for you to believe. Yet for me to accept a new suggested truth it must be held firmly in my hand. I must see and grasp it, otherwise I cannot accept it."

And so for a time the matter rested. Sandy and I turned in while Paul commenced his eight hours' vigil.

It was a changed Paul that met our view upon awaking from sleep. There was something about him that suggested release from mental strife. As though a problem, long and fiercely debated, was now solved for ever. Paul gave us no clue as to its cause until Sandy commented upon his changed appearance.

"Changed, am I?" queried he with a smile. "Yes, perhaps I am." Then he paused as though he carefully weighed some momentous proposition in his mind. Then having settled the matter, said: "I wonder if I could describe your wife, Sandy? I do not want to hurt you old man, but may I try?"

"Goodness, Paul! Have you seen her?" broke in Sandy, tremulously. "Tell me, man! Is it her, here on board?"

"All in good time, old chap," said Paul soothingly. "Let me attempt a description. Sit by the table Sandy, and you, Jim. We shall be free of danger for some hours yet. What I have to say will not take long."

We did as Paul directed, with poor old Sandy looking white and shaken. I, too, felt the strain of anticipated revelation, for Paul's attitude was charged with the positive force of convicted belief.

As Paul, with eyes closed, described her whom he conceived to be Sandy's ill-fated wife and sweetheart, Sandy's features underwent a rapid transformation. He was white and shaken at the commencement of the recital, but now his face was suffused with a glow of joy, and of unutterable happiness.

"I want no other proof, Paul, that you have seen her," said Sandy with rapture. "Just as you have described her, so was she with me on the old Earth. As I have ever believed in the continuity of existence, so I knew I should see her again. I could not determine when or where, but thought it may be after I, too, had passed through the portals of physical death. But give me the details, old man, of how and when you saw her."

"It was during the watch I have just completed," replied Paul, settling himself to tell the story. "And just as it occurred, so I will tell you.

"I must honestly confess, that, while to myself I have vehemently discountenanced the possibility of clairvoyant perception, and, openly to you the possibility of continued existence, yet, during my watch, I allowed both possibilities to occupy my mind. I did so in order to keep my mind engaged while upon observation duty. I did what so many more have done under similar circumstances – conducted a mental debate.

"First I allowed your hypothesis of universal desire and consent for the continuity of existence. Then having in mind Jim's account of clairvoyant perception, I allowed the possibility of manifestation. Then, in opposition, I marshalled all the facts known to me of science. It was naturally hard going with your fancies against my facts, when I heard a slight movement behind me.

"Thinking, perhaps, one of you was rousing, I took no notice and continued my cogitations. Again that movement came, and this time some queer sensation thrilled through my being, which caused me to turn hastily in the direction of that sound.

"To say that I was startled at what I saw would be insufficient. I became petrified – not with fear, but with a great amazement.

"A vision of radiant loveliness stood in front of me, which instantly reminded me of Henrietta Rae's 'Daphne'. Sweet as the morning dew was she, and fragrant as the violet in the clear, fresh dawn. A lovely smile wreathed her face as she slowly raised her hand and placed a finger upon her lips to enjoin silence or quietness.

"'Who are you?' I gasped, at length. Silence or no silence, I felt impelled to speak. 'Tell me your name! And yet you need not, for, of course, I am really asleep and dreaming.'

"'No, you are not asleep,' said she, smilingly. 'At least not in the way you mean – physically. You have been asleep spiritually, and in the psychic sense, too. You have housed yourself within the bleak walls of materialism to such an extent that you allow no inspiring vista of spiritual development or advancement. You see nothing beyond your physical dissolution. As your companion and leader of this expedition told you – matter sits rigidly at the base of your thinking, and because of that you have missed truth as well as happiness.'

"Even now, boys, although I was keenly enjoying the situation, I still felt it was simply a superb dream.

"'But tell me who you are,' I asked again.

"'No, I cannot tell you now,' she replied. 'I am merely a means sent to break down your stubborn materialism. Your companions need no vision. They have convictions by faith, which satisfies them so far as the continuity of life is concerned. Certainly, one of them craves for vision, but not to strengthen his conviction. It is just the humanity in him, crying out for a sight of his loved one. That in time will not be denied him.'"

"Thank God for that mercy!" broke in Sandy, with deep feeling. "But go on, old man. Tell me more! I'm sorry I interrupted."

"That's all right, Sandy, old comrade," said Paul. "I know how you feel. But to continue my narrative: 'That in time will not be denied him. As for you, dear friend, we shall probably meet again. Stay where you are. Do not move. When I depart, another will take my place. One who has been with you throughout the journey yet has been invisible to you. Farewell!'"

Chapter 14

"No sooner had she departed," continued Paul in his narrative, "then, just as she intimated, another took her place. The second, no less beautiful than the first, was somewhat shorter in stature, and, to my surprise, with a complexion like a damask rose.

"I was considerably startled by the fact that before she deigned to notice my presence, she glided to your couch, Sandy, and looked upon you with exquisite sweetness and love. I knew at once who she was, and would have wakened you, but she decidedly forbade me doing so.

"'No!' she said, and her voice was like music. 'Do not waken him. Even if you did, he would not see me. It is only given to you to see the dear one just departed and myself, because you have been so honest in your unbelief. Had your unbelief been but a pose of assumed knowledge, this revelation would have been withheld from you. I have been with you and with him' – turning and pointing to you, old man – 'and have realised all your hopes and fears. I am now about to leave him – and you. [That is to say] not merely vanish from your sight, but leave the machine entirely.'

"'For the next 70 hours you will be free of danger, but after that you must exercise the greatest possible care.'

"'When you approach within 3,500 miles of the planet, brake down your speed to one-quarter of its velocity. Continue a steady reduction until within 400 miles, then bring the controls to zero.'

"'On no account attempt to reach the planet with an oblique descent. Guide the machine in an ever-narrowing spiral until you reach the surface of the planet. One more warning! Under no circumstances must you leave the machine under a period of five terrestrial days. During that time you must open the cover of the man-tunnel gradually, admitting the atmosphere of the planet a little at a time. At the end of five terrestrial days you may disembark and your greatest discovery of all will have commenced. Fear nothing! Farewell!'

"And with one last loving look at you, Sandy, she was gone."

It was a long time before either Sandy or I could speak – Sandy because of the emotions surging through him, and I because of the astounding revelation that had been Paul's. There was no room for doubt. Paul was too sincere to imagine it had been a dream. He knew it to be an actual experience of sanity and truth, and just as he had been reluctant to accept survival after physical death, so now he gave full intellectual assent to its positiveness. There were no half measures with Paul.

After a while, Sandy mastered his emotions sufficiently for him to speak.

"I felt a keen sense of jealousy for a moment, Paul," said he with open frankness. "But thank God that feeling soon vanished. I can honestly say, now, I am glad the revelation came to you. I would give the world to see my dear one again; even now it may be my privilege. We do not know what awaits us upon Venus. Perhaps it will be there I shall see her. At any rate, old man, I have this consolation. I know what your distinguished countryman – Pasteur – cried aloud in his despair to know.

"You will remember when he lost his little child by death, he admitted he found no comfort in the abstracts of science. His great yearning was: 'I do not want limitless space, limitless time, limitless grandeur! I only want to know if somewhere and in some state the soul of my child is conscious and still sensitive to my love!' Pasteur had not the positive satisfaction that is mine. I am content to leave it there, until, perhaps, a revelation such as you had may be mine."

And, there the subject was left so far as open comment was concerned. But by the lightened feeling in my heart, and the hearty attitude of my companions, I knew we all felt the better for the great revelation that had come to us through Paul.

* * *

The seventy hours of freedom from danger, as foretold by our mysterious guest, was now up, and we commenced our preparations for descent upon the planet. We were near enough now to appreciate her growing dimensions. Her size appeared to be about equal to that of the moon from the Earth.

The unique feature about the planet that struck us was the entire absence of visible markings upon her surface. There was nothing to indicate if she was constituted similar to the Earth and contained continents and seas. It was just an unrelieved picture of whiteness.

While Sandy stood upon observational duty in front of the silvered mirror, Paul and I stood by the controls, waiting for the word of command from our leader. In a few moments he spoke.

"Stand by, boys!" came his crisp command. "Be ready with the controls immediately I speak. We seem to be very near the planet, yet I'm hanged if I can tell whether we are approaching a world like the old Earth, or whether we are running into a ball of cloud and mist. No, don't leave the control, Jim!" – as I started forward to look in the mirror.

"Neither of you leave your post for an instant. When I say 'Right!' push over the forward control to 22 degrees, advance Jim, and you, Paul, set the aft control at 60 degrees retard."

Anxiously we waited, ready to obey our chief the moment he spoke. It seemed an eternity before he issued the command. The moment he gave the signal, we each obeyed, and our speed immediately broke down to quarter full velocity, or to just over 800 miles per hour.

"Let her stay at that for a time," said Sandy. "How I wish I could see some definite feature upon the planet. It seems so weird to me."

"It's all right, old man," replied Paul soothingly. "It is a bit awesome, I'll admit. But don't forget we will come out without danger if we obey the explicit orders of our mysterious guest."

"Ah! I'd forgotten for a moment, Paul, in the feeling of such personal responsibility," said Sandy. "But don't speak of her as 'our mysterious guest': she was my wife, and, as you say, if we carry out her instructions, it will turn out well with us. Keep your hands well on the controls as we talk, and be ready to shut off the power completely when I say. What do you think of the position, Jim?"

"I don't think there is much to worry about, Sandy," I replied, "especially if we keep to the injunctions given us by her who we believe to be your wife. At the same time the whole aspect of our approach to Venus is intriguing in the extreme. Of course we know that McEwen and Sargent claimed to have detected a very obvious and rather deep indentation in the termination of the planet. But apparently both must have been misled, for even with our near proximity to Venus, we have failed to detect a single feature.

"The supposed features gave the planet an axial rotation of 23 hours and 21 minutes, which, with its smaller bulk, compares favourably with that of the Earth.

"At the same time we know that Schiaparelli, who studied the planet under the most ideal conditions, gave his opinion that Venus turned on its axis once in 224 days. That is to say, the planet, through tidal friction, has slowed down to such an extent that she ever presents the same face to the sun. If that is so, we can only dare to expect sentient life upon her sunward side.

"As to her atmosphere, we are as much in the dark now as when we commenced our voyage. In fact, so far as real observation is concerned, we seem to..."

"Look out! Good G...! Bring the controls to zero! Quick, for the love of heaven! We're in it now!"

And as Sandy uttered his quick, broken commands, we were plunged into some mysterious vapour which completely obscured our view.

Chapter 15

Never shall I forget the thrill of awesome delight that surged through my being when I first viewed the surface of the planet Venus. I need scarcely say that my companions experienced the same awesome thrill.

I anticipate some thoughtful reader of this journal, in reading the paragraph above, will be led to exclaim: "But you have led us to believe you had already seen the planet, even as every observer has seen her times and again. How, then, can you suggest this to be your first sight of Venus?" Let me explain.

We thought we had seen the planet Venus, just as astronomers upon Earth think they have seen her. But I would suggest that no observer upon Earth has ever seen, and perhaps never will see, the actual surface of the planet. And for an obvious reason. I can best explain that reason by continuing the narrative of our adventures.

When Sandy issued his crisp command to bring the controls to zero, he knew by the behaviour of the machine that we were within the gravitational pull of the planet. We needed now no motive force, seeing that the pull alone was sufficient to give us landing upon the planet's surface.

Simultaneous with the shutting-off of power, we plunged headlong into what appeared to be an opaque substance, similar to an immense fog bank. It was not only uncanny, but the situation was charged with potent dangers.

I have heard of pilots who have permanently lost their nerve through flying in what appeared to them an unending bank of fog, and some, at last, through sheer terror, have crashed to the ground, unable to stand the strain any longer.

To us the whole aspect was blotted out. It was a nerve-wracking ordeal in that we simply had to stand helplessly by and await any eventuality that might occur.

We knew – and the knowledge added to our horror – that we were rapidly descending. Instead of being upon an even keel, or having a slight deflection, we knew that the prow of our machine was almost beneath our feet. We could not bring our aft control into operation, because, through the velocity of our first descent into the pull of Venus, the aft part of the machine became at right angles to the line of contact. That is to say: the stern of our machine was at an angle of ninety degrees to the Earth.

So far as we were conscious, we had obeyed explicitly the injunctions of Sandy's wife when she appeared to Paul. Yet, to all appearances, we were doomed to disaster.

"This is getting more than I can stand," said Sandy at last, breaking a silence of terrible intensity. "I wonder if it is through the avenue of death that I shall see her; that she knew, being mortal, I could see her by no other way. If that is the case, then may death come quickly. I cannot stand this strain much longer."

"Old man," said Paul quietly, "our positions seem strangely reversed. I was the unbeliever, you were the faithful optimist. I suppose it is a law of life – or of human nature – when once an unbeliever has been converted to the truth he will go the whole hog and cease his doubts forever. I am convinced, little as I can explain the present circumstance, things will turn out right."

Paul's words proved prophetic, for scarcely had he ceased to speak when we literally shot out into glorious sunshine and perfect daylight. Far, far beneath us, we could see, for the first time, the surface of the planet. And strangely enough, with our emergence from that dreadful opaque substance, our machine righted itself and immediately swung upon an even keel. Not one of us had touched the controls, yet, just as I have indicated, so it happened. We learned later the reason of this strange occurrence.

As soon as Sandy saw the machine had righted itself, he at once took charge in order to steer it in a circular direction, giving me instructions to watch the altitude gauge. As we circled round in a huge sweep, I noticed that no change came upon the gauge, to which fact I drew Sandy's attention.

"There's only one explanation for that, Jim," said Sandy, as we watched the gauge together. "We are keeping constant to one altitude. It's very strange, yet it seems to me that some influence is ascending from the planet sufficient for the machine to resist gravitation. Then, too, there is another mystery. Our motive power is cut to zero, but we are still in motion. It..."

"Look out boys!" cried Paul, and for a second our hearts seemed to miss a beat. Even as Paul cried out, the prow of the machine deflected downwards and we dropped apparently a distance of half a mile. Immediately the machine righted itself, and we again swung round in a huge sweep upon an even keel.

There had really been no danger. It was just that momentary sickening sensation that comes to one when commencing the downward glide upon a gigantic switch-back track. Two further similar experiences came to us, for which we were more or less ready, and then to our joy we found by the altitude gauge we were slowly but surely descending.

Gradually our circles became narrower, and as we descended the presence of an appreciable atmosphere became evident. From the constant half-inch of mercury in the gauge which obtained throughout our voyage through space, it gradually ascended the columns. Two, three, six, eight inches were recorded in the tubes, and when we found, to our intense satisfaction, the mercury still rising, and with the consequent abatement of oxygen through the release valves, we turned our attention to the silvered mirror in order to feast our eyes upon the scene below.

There was no doubt in our minds now as to the physical constitution of Venus. Far below us we could see a replica of the old Earth. Continents and seas were there, and as we approached nearer the surface we saw that, just as on the Earth, there were mountains, hills and valleys.

There were many remarkable features attending our descent, to none of which could we assign a logical explanation. One surprising feature that happened to us now was the fact that we should land within the confines of a huge ringed plain. We saw that the plain was fertile, but we used every endeavour to avoid landing there because of the high mountains that completely surrounded it. We felt it would be very difficult to negotiate the sheer walls of the plain when once we had left the machine. But though we operated the controls, no answering response came. It was as though some unseen power had the machine in its grip, compelling it to take a course already assigned and fixed.

Slowly we cleared the tops of the high mountains, and then, as gracefully as a bird, our machine came to rest in the very centre of the ringed plain.

The moment we felt the soft impact of the machine with the ground, and we realised our long journey was ended, it was natural that our long-pent-up emotions held sway. I do not think any one of us have any clear recollection of the next hour. For all the world we were like three schoolboys who had witnessed the victory of their favourite school team in an all-important football match. We just clasped hands all round, danced, sang, shouted – aye, and I believe we shed tears. But what cared we for expressing our weakness to the other! Had we not achieved that which was stated to be impossible? It was a dream of distorted fancy. Foolish! Unattainable! Yet here we were, with solid conviction upon our side. Laugh those who will. We had achieved!

Chapter 16

It was a long time after our wonderful landing ere we bethought ourselves to commence the disconnecting of the man-tunnel cover. Presently our excitement abated, and we were able to give thought to the question of disembarking.

"We'll obey our instructions to the letter," was Sandy's command. "So, first of all we'll slack the cover clamps, but not attempt to move the cover for a few hours. Then we'll take a meal."

Paul and I at once responded to the dictates of our chief, and presently reported the clamps free.

"Very well, boys," said Sandy, "now we will sit at the table and have a meal. There is no need to set a watch. I do not think we shall be disturbed until a period equal to five terrestrial days has expired. I..."

"By the way," interposed Paul, "we landed in the full glare of the sun. The popular theory is, as you know, that Venus turns upon her axis once in the same period as she revolves round the sun. In other words, if this assumption is true, we shall dwell in perpetual daylight while we remain upon the planet. But where's the sun? His position will give us the solution."

It was, of course, the excitement of one experience that had prevented us from noticing any phenomenon save the fact that we had arrived upon Venus. We now turned our attention to the silvered mirror, and a brief observation revealed to us the sun was declining from the meridian.

"No!" I exclaimed. "We shall not be in perpetual daylight! Don't you see what the sun tells us? Venus is revolving upon an axis similar to the Earth. The old controversy is ended. We have discovered that which has ever been hidden from terrestrial observers. Daylight and darkness will be our experience just as we experienced upon the old Earth."

"And have you noticed another significant fact?" observed Paul, with a look of extreme puzzlement upon his face. "That opaque belt through which we came, and which caused us such terror, is not visible. It's very queer. We ought to see it, because to us it is an elementary fact that it lies between us and the sun."

It certainly was strange, yet it was just as Paul had stated. The sun was much larger than when viewed from the Earth, and his clear, round disc revealed no intervening mist or obstruction. Yet we knew it did exist, seeing we had but recently passed through it. The thing was strangely inexplicable. Try as we would, we could come to no logical explanation. Finally we had to abandon the problem as being altogether beyond our powers of solution. When, later, we knew the cause, we saw how necessary and natural it was.

That evening gave us the most wonderful sunset we had ever witnessed. In process of time we got to appreciate its wonderful diversity of colour, but on that first evening of our arrival its infinite grandeur was too much for our untrained eyes. Through some unknown physical cause, the light from the dying sun was so lit up as though it had passed through some gigantic prism. The whole heavens became one huge rainbow, and the colours, reflecting to the surface of the planet, caused the plain and the surrounding mountains to be alight with its several shades.

As the sun finally set, our wonder and awe grew apace. The whole vault of heaven became ablaze with stars. Clearer, and with their intrinsic value enhanced, we saw the constellations with which we were familiar. And, too, we saw the planet Mercury as we could never hope to see him from the Earth. There came a time when we had the opportunity of viewing the night sky through one of the powerful telescopes possessed by the Venusian astronomers. When we did, the sight afforded us was one we shall never forget. But... I must not anticipate.

As we prepared for bed, Sandy voiced the opinion of us all in saying how good it was to lie restful with no thought of danger. For ten months, we had kept a prolonged vigil. There was no single period of the journey when one or the other of us wasn't stationed upon observation duty. As the reader instinctively must know, it had been a strain. Even as we slept in turn, the sleep was often fitful. But now, for the first time in ten months, we could sleep with restful repose. So deep was that first period of rest that when we awoke, the sun was was high in the heavens.

After breakfast we moved the cover of the man-tunnel so that we could begin to modify the atmosphere in the machine. And here we almost met with tragedy of a terribly malignant character. So peculiar was its nature that I wish to record it in detail.

It was but a little way we moved the cover, just sufficient to allow a thin ray of light to penetrate the dark recess of the man-tunnel. Paul and I then returned to the living room, leaving Sandy in the shaft of the tunnel. No harm suggested itself, to me at least, and while I entered up the log, Paul took a careful survey of the entrancing Venusian landscape through the silvered mirror. I did not notice the passage of time, as the details of the log engaged my whole attention, and I was considerably startled when Paul suddenly exclaimed: "I say, Jim, I wonder what's keeping old Sandy?"

"Good heavens, Paul! You startled me," said I. "Keeping him? Curiosity I expect. I should have stayed a little longer in the shaft, too, but for having to enter up the log. What can keep him but just the curiosity of noting the effect of the intermingling of the two atmospheres? I am a little curious, too, let's go and find him."

"One minute, Jim," said Paul, and as I looked at him, I saw his face had gone white as death. "When we moved the cover and that thin ray of light penetrated the shaft, did you experience any extraordinary sensation? Any feeling of apprehension, I mean?"

"No, I did not!" I answered, somewhat mystified by Paul's attitude. "But what is the matter? Are you ill?"

"I'm certainly not ill," said Paul, with a shaky laugh, "and I expect it is just fancy, but when we moved the cover and the outside air of Venus began to mingle with the inside air of our machine, I felt for the moment we were in the presence of some evil influence – some evil and malignant spirit, if you like. But the moment I reached the living room, I felt quite normal.

"I should have mentioned that queer feeling to you, but was just a trifle afraid of appearing ridiculous. You know I have ever been a pronounced materialist until I had that revelation from Sandy's spirit wife, and... well... somehow I now seem to be strangely alive to psychic influence."

"Then come along, man, come along," I answered apprehensively. "There may be some reason for such a feeling. God grant that no harm has overtaken Sandy."

We quickly made our way to the shaft of the man-tunnel, and discovered to our consternation that Paul's fears were only too well-founded.

Sandy was writhing upon the platform of the tunnel as though he wrestled with a human antagonist, and seemed well nigh spent. His breath came in sobbing gasps, while the veins of his forehead protruded like knotted cords.

Aghast at such a spectacle, I sprang to his side, imploring him with incoherent cries to tell me his trouble.It was lucky for me that Paul was immediately behind. When Sandy felt human arms about him, his failing strength revived, and as he gripped my throat, he would have strangled me, had not Paul torn his hands away. With a quick turn of the wrist, Paul clenched his hand and struck Sandy a lightning blow upon the point of his chin. With a groan Sandy fell to the ground, unconscious.

"Quick, Jim!" panted Paul. "It was the only way. Grasp his legs. We'll soon get him out of this damned place. Quick, man! Into the living room!"

Chapter 17

We carried Sandy into the living room and laid him upon the floor.

"Mad as a hatter!" was Paul's terse remark, wiping the perspiration from his face. "No, Jim, you need not tie his legs. He'll be all right here, I fancy. Get some brandy from the locker, there's a good fellow. No! Don't get it from the fore-cabin – we'll need to discuss this little affair before venturing beyond the living room. That's it! Now give it to me. Come on, old Sandy top!" – and though Paul had been the strict medico, his appellation hid a volume of fears. "Come on, old Sandy, get this down you!"

With infinite tenderness, he raised Sandy's head, and gently poured the brandy between his lips. Anxiously I watched the process, and in a moment Sandy gave a gasp and struggled into a sitting position.

"Where am I?" he whispered, weakly. Then, as memory revived, a look of horror came into his eyes. "Who?..."

"All right, old fellow," said Paul, soothingly. "Don't worry now. You are safe with Jim and I. Lie down and sleep."

"But..."

"All in good time, Sandy. Go to sleep!" And Paul, with authority in his tones, but with gentleness in his actions, pressed Sandy back upon the cushion I had placed under his head.

With a sigh of extreme tiredness, Sandy closed his eyes and slept.

When Paul saw he was finally settled, he gave me a silent gesture and we retired to the other side of the living room.

"Jim," whispered he. "We are up against a stiff proposition, if I mistake not. I don't understand it, but I'm convinced Sandy encountered the same sinister influence with which I also met; that of which I told you previous to our finding him. Just what it can be I am unable to fathom. Perhaps Sandy will be able to throw some light upon it when he recovers.

"What on earth can it be?" I asked, with a feeling of irritation. "I thought our troubles over, but it seems we are still in the thick of them. I don't care a tinker's cuss for what is visible, but an invisible something of malevolency is enough to put the wind up one. Perhaps old Sandy will not care to talk of it."

"I trust he will," replied Paul. "However much it may hurt him, he is the only one to lead us to a solution."

It was with a feeling of devout thankfulness that we found Sandy, upon awakening, to be almost his old self again. When Paul put his question to him, Sandy visibly shrank from it.

"I'm infinitely sorry to trouble you, old man," said Paul, "but if this menace is to be common to all three, we ought to know something of its operation. I may say that I, too, felt a queer thrill pass through me when we removed the cover, but when we got to the living room it had passed."

"Yes, boys, I think perhaps it will be best if I give you the details of what happened."

And so Sandy braced himself to tell his story. Paul, seeing the action and knowing the telling was to be difficult, gave him a drop of neat stimulant.

"I stayed behind in the shaft," he began, "in order to see what was the effect of the intermingling atmospheres. I knew no great change could take place because we moved the cover so little. Still, I thought there may be a change enough to detect. I had not remained more than a few seconds when I found a most queer sensation stealing over my whole being. I knew at once that it was not a question of air modification, because my respiration was in no way impaired. I could breathe just as easily as before the cover was touched.

"It may sound foolish to you, but that thin ray of light filled me with a tremendous fascination. It operated upon me just as I believe a powerful psychic influence would do. That strange feeling should have warned me, and I ought to have left the shaft there and then, and rejoined you in the living room. I felt, however, you would have laughed at me had I done so; that you would have declared the excitement of landing upon Venus had gone to my head. And so I stayed on. I tried to get a grip upon myself, but for one mad moment I had a desire to throw the cover off entirely. It was a terrible struggle, and despite its zeal, I tried to argue against such madness.

"I did not know definitely, but instinctively I felt that if I removed the cover then death would overtake our little company. Through my warring senses I realised that the conditions given to Paul in the vision were imperative. It would take five terrestrial days of gradual balancing the atmospheres before our lungs would be fit to stand wholly the rarer atmosphere of Venus. I struggled hard and sanity prevailed, preventing me from throwing off the cover.

"I thought then the victory was won – fool that I was. No sooner had I resisted the desire to throw off the cover, than... (but don't laugh, boys, for God's sake, it was terribly real)... some sinister influence surrounded me. Not a vague something, but a personality. There was no articulate sound, yet the very air vibrated with menace. It seemed to vibrate 'I'll kill you! I'll kill you! You poor, puny mortal. Never shall you be reunited to her!'

"I had no time to gather any significance from the vibrations, for at that moment I felt a grip upon my throat. I fought like a wildcat, but still that tenacious grip held me. Then, just as I had given up in despair, the grip relaxed.

"Again, I can only describe that which followed as vibrations. There was no tone except that it was one of impervious insistence. 'Go to the living room,' it vibrated. 'Your life depends upon instant flight from the shaft!'

"I turned to comply, feeling that was the safest thing to do, when I felt once more that terrible grip upon my throat. I am afraid I then lost control of myself. The horror of the position dazed me. I could get no hold upon that which menaced me. I fought the fight of despair.

"Somehow I seem to remember that I could feel arms and a grip about me. Something that was solid and tangible. I believe I tried to grapple with those arms, but a terrific smash came upon my chin and I remember no more. My next conscious moment was feeling a stimulant between my lips, and finding you two bending over me. I feel almost myself again now, but what in heaven's name can be the meaning of it?"

"Thank you for telling us the details, old man," said Paul upon the conclusion of Sandy's terrible narrative. "As to what is the meaning of it, then that is what we must find out before we dare venture farther. One thing: I think we are fairly safe from that invisible peril here. Yet if we have to remain in the living room our visit to Venus comes to an abrupt termination. If that be the case, we had better consider a return to the Earth."

"No!" I exclaimed. "After all we have been through, do not let us think of an immediate return to the Earth. There must be some way out of the trouble. Cannot we get into communication with one of the Venusian wireless stations and beg for advice? Surely the menace must be known to them. Let..."

"Boys!" cried Sandy, excitedly. "Do you remember what I told you? I could not think for the moment, but now I see it clearly. That malevolent influence is against me, and me only. Venus must be the sphere upon which my wife dwells, and that malignant spirit which is preventing me from joining her. 'I'll kill you!' it said. And..."

"No, Sandy. That cannot be the case," interposed Paul. "For death itself could be no bar to rejoining your wife. Rather would it be an instantaneous help. No, there must be some other reason. In the meanwhile, let us carry out Jim's suggestion, and get in touch with a Venusian wireless station. They will surely give us advice and help."

Chapter 18

Thank God I can write of release from the horror recorded in the last chapter. With all our hearts we trust there will be no recurrence of its malignant power. We do not know, even yet, who or what Sandy's invisible antagonist was. All that we do know is that for the time being we are immune from its influence. And for that mercy we are grateful.

The knowledge of our release came from an unexpected source. Sandy acted upon my suggestion and tried to get in touch with one of the Venusian wireless stations. This was done in order to secure advice or aid to combat the insidious menace in the shaft of the man-tunnel. Every attempt, however, proved abortive. At last, overcome by vexation, Sandy turned from the microphone and commenced pacing to and fro the floor of the chart-room.

Suddenly the interior of the machine was suffused with an iridescent light. So powerful did it prove that for the moment we were held as in a trance. No form was visible, yet from the midst of those variegated hues there came a voice soft as the south wind, and soothing as a healing balm. "There is no need for further fear," said the voice. "The trouble which menaced you is removed for the time being. In the fullness of time, you will again experience its influence. At that moment it will be revealed to you how you may overcome [its sway]. Fear nothing! Farewell!"

As the voice ceased, the light vanished, and the normal reigned once more.

"Thank God that's over," said Sandy, with a quick recovery of spirits. "Now, boys, we can go to the shaft without fear and remove the cover a little farther."

Although we each knew the menace gone, I think none of us could scarce forbear a shudder as we reached the platform of the man-tunnel. Under Sandy's supervision we pushed back the cover until he called upon us to stop.

As day succeeded day, we found the internal air of the machine becoming much less dense, and the modification, of course, produced an effect upon our respiration. We found we needed to breathe slower and deeper in order to inhale the amount of oxygen necessary to our constitution. There came a time when we found it second nature to so breathe, but until we reached that stage we experienced a slight pain in the lungs. The pain proved our sentinel, for it became accentuated if we forgot and breathed quickly and lightly as was our custom upon Earth.

Upon the termination of the stipulated period (five days, to be exact), we had everything ready for disembarking. Before leaving the machine we took the precaution of closing the oxygen release valves and locking them. This we did for a very obvious reason. The atmosphere of Venus was considerably less in pressure than was the oxygen stored in the tanks. Therefore, the valves, being purely automatic, and controlled inversely by outside pressure, there would be a continuous waste of the precious gas reserved for the return journey. We dared not forget that upon the completion of our sojourn upon Venus, a ten months' voyage through the void lay ahead of us. We did not know whether there were means upon Venus to re-charge the tanks, hence we took no risks of losing the store still remaining therein.

Each strapped upon his back a supply of concentrated food and drink, and we were ready for what Venus had to offer. Sandy, as leader of the expedition, had the honour of being the first to leave the machine. Paul followed, and I emerged at last.

It may be a point of honour to be in the van-guard, but there are times when it is a distinct advantage in being in the rear. The present circumstances proved its truth. As my head and shoulders emerged from the man-tunnel, I was just in time to see Sandy's legs up in the air with Paul doing a graceful swallow dive after him. The sight was too much for my gravitas, and I laughed until the tears rolled down my face.

As I ascended higher, I saw Sandy sprawled upon the grass with Paul stretched by his side. Both had such a comical look of wonderment upon their faces that it started me off again. But, oh! the old adage: "He who laughs last," etc. In the midst of my laughter, both feet shot from under me, and I also took a header through the air.

Paul was just regaining his feet when I landed plump upon his shoulders, and down he went again, with me atop.

"Damn your clumsiness, Jim!" cried Paul, throwing me from him. "Why the devil can't you leave the machine like a gentleman instead of slithering into me like a thunderbolt? Sandy and I alighted with grace and dignity, but of course you must want just the little bit of ground I already claimed as mine. I was just going to give it up to you, but, no! You couldn't wait until there was vacant possession. You must butt in."

"I'm glad it was you and not me, Paul," said Sandy, laughing heartily. "I expect our exit did look graceful and dignified to Jim. But what his very own exit looked like to me when he butted into you simply baffles description."

It was the first real fun we had experienced since the commencement of our flight, and we enjoyed it to the full.

There was little need to question the cause of our hurried exit from the machine. It was entirely due to the first general inhalation of the rarer atmosphere of Venus. The effect was not long sustained; just a temporary giddiness – which caused our dive through the air – and we were ourselves again.

The morning was glorious in the extreme. The Sun was an hour high in the heavens, and the soft carpet of grass beneath our feet, with flowers scattered indiscriminately around, made the commencement of our journey a very joyous one. Our feelings were too deep for speech. We simply walked along and drank in the magnificent vista around.

"It's those mountains ahead that are bothering me," said Sandy, at last breaking the silence. "The air is somewhat difficult here in the plain, and I am afraid it will be too attenuated for us up there."

"Probably there's a pass through them at ground level," suggested Paul. "If the plain is entirely surrounded, with no cleavage or gorge, how is it the plain has not become an inland sea or lake? To me it looks strangely like snow on the top of that big fellow to the left. And yes, look! Why, there are several around the plain that are snowcapped. The water flowing down as the snow melts must find an outlet somewhere. Otherwise, as I suggested a moment ago, the plain would be a lake. Then look at the grass and flowers! The soil must be generously served with moisture, either rain or dew – more probably rain – and unless there is an underground reservoir into which the rain percolates, that, too, must find an outlet. The strange feature is that so far as we can see there is not a single stream in the whole of this vast plain."

Another hour's walk and we were at the foot of those gigantic mountains. No second glance was needed to tell us that, so far as we were concerned, those mountains were impregnable and inaccessible. There was nothing else to do but begin a search for a possible outlet.

Chapter 19

Just as Paul anticipated, we found an outlet from the ringed plain. We also found trouble. Looking back upon that episode, although shame and contrition came to each of us at the time, I do not see we were altogether blameworthy. We were, after all, Earth dwellers – with terrestrial appetites, instincts, and experiences. It came about in this way.

When we arrived at the foot of the mountains, Sandy directed Paul to survey the right and myself the left.

There was little fear of being lost, seeing that the whole area of the plain was within our view. He who found an outlet was to heliograph the fact to the others by means of a pocket mirror each carried. Sandy was to remain mid-distance, waiting for the signal.

It must have been an hour afterwards when I heard a faint "Hello!" and, turning, I saw the flash of Paul's mirror signalling he had found the outlet.

When Sandy and I joined him, we saw not only the gorge, but a beautiful, broad stream of water, fed by rushing torrents from the foot of the mountains. We found, later, that natural conduits conveyed the waters from all round the plain to this solitary gorge. But while the greater portion flowed in a broad river to the sea, nature had so decreed that moisture should find its way through the soil to every part of the ringed plain. Hence its continuous life and beauty.

Simultaneously we ran to the side of the river and took a deep draught of its clean, cold water.

"Ah!" exclaimed Paul, raising his voice above the din of rushing water. "That drink was excellent. If we could only find a bird or a rabbit? What a jolly old dinner we'd have."

"Yes, old man," I answered. "That would suit my palate, too. We've had nothing but concentrated food for ten months, and a little fresh meat now would send me into an ecstasy of delight. I wonder if there are game laws existing here? Even if there are, then I think I should violate them. What say you, Sandy?"

"That I would!" responded Sandy, smacking his lips in mock anticipation of a juicy joint, or of picking a wishbone. "Whatever code of game laws exist here, I think I'd do a month for a brace of pheasants broiling over a clear wood fire. But, boys, even suppose we saw a bird or hare, what weapons have we to kill them?"

As there appeared no likelihood of game – bird or animal – appearing, we partook of concentrated food and continued our journey.

We followed the river through the gorge for about five miles, and then there opened up to our view a glorious landscape, very similar to what we knew of the old Earth. We could follow the windings of the river, growing ever broader, until it was lost in the distance. Away on either side of us were tree-crowned hills, while, in the centre distance, we saw something that caused our hearts to beat with tumultuous joy. The sun shone upon some substance which appeared to resemble glass, and we saw that a city of considerable extent lay ahead of us.

We had scarcely noted these wonders when we were startled by hearing a swish of wings, and there, right before us, six or seven birds – somewhat larger than pigeons – alighted. They appeared to take not the slightest notice of us, and continued feeding as though we were miles away.

"Here we are, boys!" cried Sandy in excited delight. "A piece of rock each, a careful aim and three birds are ours. Quick! And don't for heaven's sake miss!"

Sandy's aim was true, and his bird fell dead. Paul's aim and mine were not so true, and we had the mortification of seeing our birds scampering away, crying in the agony of their hurt. The birds untouched ceased feeding, and raised their heads apparently in wonder at the cries of their wounded comrades. We took little heed of these. The lust to capture and kill led us to chase the wounded ones, which, after an exciting chase, we captured.

It was the work of a few moments to pluck and draw our prizes, and soon we had them cooking over a fire. The other birds had now flown away.

We were about to commence our attack upon the appetising food when there came a swift rush of air, and something alighted gracefully near to our camp. Not the slightest noise accompanied the descent, yet here before us was nothing if not an aeroplane. To prove its truth, there stepped from the machine a young man, as splendidly proportioned as ever had been my lot to see.

We sprang to our feet to give him welcome, but as I looked into his eyes, I at once became alarmed. It was not a look of temper or fury in his eyes. I can best describe it as a blaze of righteous indignation. When he spoke, his voice was controlled and exquisitely modulated – yet each word cut like the lash of a whip.

"So this is what you would do!" said he, in faultless English, with quiet scorn. "Have you Earth dwellers realised the terrible import of your action? For the first time in the history of this, our world, you have brought pain and anguish to one of our creatures. Were you not wise enough to see that the lack of fear upon the part of these creatures was proof that hitherto alarm and dread, as such, was unknown to them? Why, then...?"

"I am exceedingly sorry if my friends and I have killed birds of a tamed and domesticated stock," interrupted Sandy, stung into retort by the attitude of our visitor. "But seeing they were flying free in open country, we thought they could not be birds of private ownership. If, of course, we have violated your game laws, we must be judged by those laws. At the same time – and of this you are probably aware – for ten months we have had no chance of a change of diet. What more natural then, seeing the opportunity, we embraced it."

Although Sandy had been unpardonably precipitate in breaking in upon our visitor's censure of our conduct, he courteously listened to the end.

"You must distinctly understand," said he, slowly and with emphasis, "you are now in a world of a totally different constitution from that of which you are native. Fortunately for you I am acquainted with your voyage, and with the whole constitution of your world – Terra. Such terms as 'tamed,' 'game laws', and even your interpretation of 'domesticated' and 'private ownership', are foreign to our constitution. Each term in its basic principle is contrary to the laws laid down by the Master of the Spheres. This, to you, is difficult to understand. Presently it will all be made clear. This, however, you must understand and obey: under no circumstances must you attempt a repetition of to-day's conduct. As it is, the creatures you killed by wounding are forfeit, and even now are beyond your powers to consume."

As we turned to the fire, we found it as our strange visitor intimated. Every trace of bird – body and feathers – had vanished as though the scene of the slaughter had never occurred.

Sandy held out his hand and tendered our sincere regrets for our conduct. "At the same time," said he, "had we a Venusian guide when we started, it would never have happened. That is our present need – a guide."

"And that is the reason for my presence," responded our visitor, as a smile flitted across his face. "I intended meeting you an hour earlier, but was detained. Let the episode of your cruelty be the last you attempt. One other and you must return at once to Terra."

Chapter 20

With the advent of the guide – whose name we found to be Eueun – our further adventures upon Venus became fascinating in the extreme. Eueun proved a capital fellow, with a fund of humour that won our hearts. He was not of a boisterous nature, but he ever evinced a keen pleasure in pulling our legs. With our experience of Earth life, we were naturally greenhorns amidst the totally different constitution of Venus. An account of our first all-night camp under the starry skies will reveal the humorous character of our guide. The joke was certainly against us; nevertheless, I will recount it.

As the Sun sank to rest, Sandy suggested making camp for the night where we were. As it seemed a good spot, we commenced to gather brushwood in order to make a blazing fire.

"Why are you making up the fire?" asked Eueun with interest. "You will find little difference in the temperature between day and night in these latitudes."

"Well, it's a comfort to know that," replied Sandy. "One reason surely was for warmth, but the more important reason is that being in the open country there is little fear of wild beasts attacking with the fire going."

"Ah, yes, true," said Eueun. "You see, I am of the city. Your sagacity is worthy of notice."

As the fire flamed up, I thought I detected a smile upon Eueun's face. But as no significance of that smile commended itself to me, I let it fade from my mind.

With the utmost magnanimity Eueun requested Sandy to continue the leadership of the party, while he himself would act as guide and interpreter. Hence, following the usual custom of our Earth life, Sandy set the watches for the night. He would take the first watch, Paul the second, and I the third. As Eueun had declared, his life was of the city, Sandy exempted him from sentinel duties.

"Thank you. That is good of you," said Eueun, with solemn emphasis. "Yes, I do feel somewhat sleepy. Keep a sharp lookout, and if you see anything of an untoward nature, call me at once. I'll be better fitted, perhaps, in guiding you to safety.

What fools we were to be sure! Feeling that all was snug, and with Sandy on watch, the rest of us settled down to sleep. Nothing happened during the first two watches, and when Paul roused me, I shook the sleep from my eyes and took his place. How awesome and lonely was the night. The very stillness oppressed me and sent a shiver down my spine. I peered into the surrounding gloom and satisfied myself that all was well.

Towards morning, just before it became light, I let the fire die down. Soon the light of the sun was visible across the countryside, and at that moment I heard a sound from a near-by bush. To my dismay I saw a huge brown head surrounded by a shaggy mane.

"Wake! Boys!" I cried. "There's a wild beast close upon us!"

Instantly there was an excited bustle. We had no weapons, and as the fire was now no longer a protection, we were more or less defenceless.

"Quick!" cried Eueun. "Make for the bushes to the right!"

"No! No!" yelled Sandy. "Why, man alive, that's almost near to the brute!

Look! There behind us! There are trees with boughs low down. Make each for one, and climb for your lives!"

Even as he spoke, the creature uttered an ear-splitting roar, and away we sprinted for the trees. In his haste, Sandy caught his foot in some obstacle and over he went. Paul, not seeing him stumble, fell over him. And I, no whit less fortunate, sprawled over the two.

Scrambling to our feet, we saw to our horror the beast coming towards us. In my terror I bumped into Paul and sent him cannoning into Sandy, and again we were all mixed up on the ground. Things began to look desperate when we were startled to see Eueun rolling upon the ground and laughing so immoderately that I began to think the excitement had been too much for him.

"Ho! ho! ha! ha! ha!" laughed he. "Quick! You'll never reach those trees if you keep mixing yourselves up on the ground."

There was something so comically taunting in the laughter and advice that we began to feel exceedingly foolish. We felt more so when we saw Eueun walk over to the beast and stroke his broad head.

"That's a new experience for you, old fellow," said he as he patted the beast's head. "You've never seen a more dignified flight or a more glorious scramble as you have witnessed to-day. It's been jolly, old fellow, has it not?"

And then Eueun sobered down. "After all," said he, "it was rather a mean trick to play upon you seeing you knew no different."

"You have tamed this creature then?" queried Sandy, lamely.

"There you go again!" exclaimed Eueun with a smile upon his lips. 'Tamed'? No, it is certainly not 'tamed'. As I understand your meaning of the verb 'to tame', it presupposes a wild, savage state. The history of our world knows no such state. Every creature upon this globe is free and unfettered, and is the fearless companion of man. I ought to have told you this last evening as you prepared the fire and set the watches. But the joke was too good to forego. Still, as it was only intended as fun, you will forgive me, I know."

Of course we forgave him, and joined in the laugh against ourselves. It must have been a rich experience for him as he watched us light the protective fire, and Sandy mount guard, over a dangerous camp. We made friends with the beast, which, after allowing us to stroke his tawny head, trotted off into the bush.

"But why is the constitution of your planet so different from that of ours?" asked Paul, after a pause. "To us, the experience of yesterday and that which we have just passed through, are commonplace. We kill for food, and we kill for sport. Between the wild things of Earth and man there is eternal fear and hatred. Your life here seems to be the antithesis of Earth life."

"And so it is the antithesis of Earth life," replied Eueun earnestly. "Listen! The difference is so great that were I to tell you all now it would mentally derange you. You must be patient, and as you are able to bear it, so it will be revealed to you. At the same time I am permitted to reveal only material differences. The difference in our higher constitution will be shown you by Mentor, the chief of our teachers. But I expect you will be needing breakfast, will you not?"

We agreed as to the need, but had now become heartily sick of concentrated food. Eueun evidently read our thoughts. He smiled with reassurance and went over to his machine, from which he returned with several packages.

"You are tired of your usual fare, I know," said he. "See, I have brought you something which will assuage your hunger and, at the same time, satisfy your palate."

Visions of cold roast chicken rose before my eyes, and if the same vision rose before the eyes of my companions, then the vision proved a mirage.

"Ah!" exclaimed Eueun with a certain amount of sadness in his tones as he saw our disappointed expressions. "You thought it meat – otherwise known as 'flesh' food. Eat this and enjoy it, for there will be no flesh food given you here!"

Chapter 21

However much we may have been disappointed at the fact that our food would not be of flesh, we thoroughly enjoyed the repast. Until that moment I think neither of us had any idea how satisfying to hunger and pleasant to palate a vegetarian diet could be.

The full menu of that first breakfast we had upon Venus consisted of eggs, wholemeal bread (with the most nutritious butter I have tasted), fruit, nutmeat, cream cheese, and concluding with rice balls in cream. For drink we had milk, rich and sustaining, or wine of the grape produce. I may say here that though the wine was of a lively character, it was only so to us. This point I must enlarge later. Sufficient for the moment, Eueun made it his special business to see we drank sparingly.

We felt renewed beings after such a delightful meal, and with buoyant step we walked over to Eueun's machine to examine it. We found to our surprise that it was made entirely of metal, similar to that of which our own machine was constructed.

"Yes," said Eueun smilingly, in answer to our several queries, "my machine is made from a very light but tenacious metal called 'manganfoil'. It is an alloy, of course, and much lighter than that of which your machine is constructed. I..."

"But you have not seen our machine," interrupted Sandy. "How, then, can you know its construction?"

"We'll let it go at that," replied Eueun, smiling enigmatically. "All the same, I do know! But let me continue my answers to your queries. My machine is devoid of wings or propellers – even as your machine is devoid of them. You are years ahead of your contemporaries, and have discovered a motive power which has been known to us for centuries – that of velocified magnetism. When, in the years to come, terrestrial posterity discovers this power, they will find that high velocities can be attained not only through your denser atmosphere, but also over your railroads and through your seas.

"But, come, you not only wish to know things – you also wish to see. Stay here a few moments while I take my single-seater, and I will return shortly with an aerodecker."

Easy as a ray of light, Eueun shot into the air. No sound attended the ascent, and soon his machine was beyond our vision.

"Well, we are certainly progressing," said Paul, after Eueun had departed. "And if I mistake not, our future discoveries will be along the lines of more startling wonders. This seems to be intimated in the fact that Eueun is to show us only material differences. What is reserved for Mentor to show us, I dare not even conjecture."

Before Sandy or I could make any comment, we saw a large machine approaching, out of which, as it touched the ground, Eueun sprang. Two huge rockers were beneath this wonderful machine, upon which it landed without jolt or shock.

In the descent, the machine alighted upon the fore part of the rockers, and instantly rocked back to its centre of gravity, where it remained perfectly poised. On the ascending flight, the machine rocked slightly back-wards, with the stern deflected, and the prow inclined, ready to take the air.

The machine itself was constructed upon lines similar to an up-to-date privately owned yacht. There was a spacious promenade deck, beneath which were dining, reading and sleeping cabins.

To Eueun's smiling invitation we quickly responded, and were soon on deck. With a "Hayho!" to some invisible personage, the machine was in the air. Knowing the machine rocked backwards in the ascending flight, I instinctively grasped a support. But there was no need for my hasty action, for the outer shell was free of the deck – the deck swinging upon centre bearings.

As we ascended higher, Eueun called us below, where, in the reading cabin, he pointed to three peculiarly shaped head-dresses.

"Put these on," said he, "or you will be suffocated up here. It is not easy for you to breathe in the lower levels of our atmosphere. Up here will be impossible for you."

In the few minutes he had been talking, we certainly found respiration growing more difficult. The moment our head-dresses were affixed, we found relief. Each apparatus was so constructed that while oxygen was supplied freely, no bar was put upon our powers to converse. Having donned the head-dresses we went again on deck.

The power and observation room was at the forepart of the machine, and here we were introduced to the pilot. He was about 45 years of age and a really fine specimen of a man. It needed little powers of observation to see there was equal status between the pilot and Eueun.

With perfect composure and frankness, he held out his hand to us in salutation. Knowing the rigid lines of demarcation separating social orders upon Earth, I questioned Eueun and bluntly asked him if the pilot was "his man".

"*My man*?" said he, with a bantering smile. "Yes, I suppose he is – and at the same time I am his man."

"That is rather a paradox, Eueun, is it not?" asked Paul, who had heard my query. "I take it you are the owner of this machine and your man is the pilot. In other words, to make use of distinctions as we understand them, he is your servant."

"Then you must understand different," replied Eueun, pleasantly but earnestly. "It will take you a long time to assimilate our standards because, as I have told you already, they are the antitheses of your standards. I find it difficult to explain further, seeing that such explanations involve trespassing into Mentor's domain.

"It is he who will make this clear to you. Sufficient for me to say at the moment, I certainly own this machine as every person native to this globe may own one, if their capacity, inclination and desire so permits.

"And Trilus is the pilot because, firstly, it is his capacity – or, if you will, his niche in the scheme of things. And, secondly, it is his pleasure.

"But Mentor will explain this to you more fully. He will also explain how Nature checks over-production in all life's ramifications, and normalises the demand in capacities, inclinations and desires.

"But come! If we talk here too long, you will miss the sights I wish to show you."

We wandered at will for four days, speeding at high velocity across the north polar regions, then at slower speed around the tropical and sub-tropical zones. Eueun told us that all human life was confined within the limits of the north and south temperate zones.

Confined within this wide range, we saw many towns and cities. From our exalted height, we could appreciate the exquisite design of their lay-out.

Each town and city was planned with geometrical precision. In shape each was a perfect circle, at the centre of which was a wide, open circular space. Radiating from the centre were broad arterial roads, intersected by other roads, equally broad, in ever-widening circles to the boundary of the city or town.

While each residential house had its own playing lawn, on the outer edge of the city or town were also large and commodious playing fields. Business houses, factories, and all houses of commerce were situated on sites right away from the residential cities and towns, and as transport was brought to a fine art of speed and comfort, distance made no difference to the day's work.

Hill and dale were resplendent with tree and flower, waving corn and vegetable produce, while, upon the seas, we saw huge ships that moved across the waters at incredible speeds.

After four days we came back to our starting point, and, with Eueun as guide, began a pilgrimage to the chief city of science and knowledge.

Chapter 22

Eueun sent back his aerodecker with the pilot, intimating to us that the tramp to the city would be beneficial and full of interest. And truly we found it so.

Passing across the river in a launch, we entered a forest of luxuriant beauty. Our sensations were indescribable as we saw the beasts (which upon Earth are wild and ferocious) docile and gentle in their demeanour.

One scene in particular arrested our attention to such a degree that it was with difficulty we tore ourselves from the spot. We were passing a grassy knoll when Sandy cried out in ecstatic delight, pointing to something at the foot of the knoll.

A huge furry cat, the very facsimile of a terrestrial tigress, was lying prone upon the grass, while two tiny balls of fur gambolled around her. As they played, the mother watched them with conscious maternal pride.

"A pretty sight, is it not?" asked Eueun, seeing our intense interest. "Come along, there is no need for fear!" And Eueun went to the mother, stroked her head, and beckoned to follow.

With remembrances of Earth conditions still ripe in our thoughts, we approached nearer with a certain amount of trepidation. But Eueun laughingly caught up one of the cubs and handed it to Sandy. The cub nestled in his arms, then raised its little head, rubbing it against Sandy's face. Paul, seeing there was no danger, picked up the other cub, but, seeing the mother rise and come towards him, hastily put it on the ground again. There was no need of fear, however, for it was not anger with which the tigress approached. If her eyes interpreted anything, it was just a parental concern for her offspring. Paul picked up the cub again and fondled it, even as I did the same.

So fascinated were we at this wonderful exhibition of docility that Eueun had the utmost difficulty in persuading us to continue the journey.

"Do you realise what we have been permitted to witness, boys?" asked Sandy, earnestly, as we walked away. "We have seen an old prophecy fulfilled. I will quote the sense if I fail at the actual words. I believe it is found in the Book of Ezekiel: "The wolf and the lamb shall dwell in harmony, and the kid and the leopard shall be friends. The calf and the young lion shall lie down together and a little child shall lead them. The unweaned child shall play with the asp, and the weaned child shall touch the adder without fear of hurt!"

(NB. Sandy meant the Prophetic Book of Isaiah, X1. 6-9. His interpretation was excellent, seeing he quoted from memory – GEH)

As Sandy quoted the above, I saw a peculiar light radiate from Eueun's eyes. His lips parted to speak, but evidently thinking better of it, he said nothing.

"Not quite fulfilment, Sandy," said Paul reflectively. "Certainly we have seen the perfect concord between man and beast, but would a little child be safe, say, alone with the family we have just left?"

"Yes," answered Eueun decisively. "The beasts do not enter the towns and cities, but roam the forests and glades around. The children ramble at will through the same forests and glades. Where we are now would be much too far from the city for a toddler to ramble. But should it do so, and, feeling tired, lay down to sleep by yon tigress and cubs, it would be as snug and safe as though it was in its own little cot at home.

"The names of our beasts are different from yours, but I will call them by the names you understand. Presently you will see a literal fulfilment of your leader's quotation – the wolf and the lamb in friendly companionship.

"We have serpents here even as you have upon Earth. It is true when I tell you that a little child may sleep within the coils of a python without fear or harm. And why should you not realise that these things ought to be?

"Your leader... may I call you Sandy? Thank you. Sandy quoted from one of your ancient books. But think back to the Genesis of that wonderful library. Does it not say there – speaking of the creation – 'Let man have dominion over fish, fowl, cattle, creeping things, and over everything that moveth upon the Earth'? It does! Well then, that is the state wished for by the Master of the Spheres.

"Unfortunately, even here your idea of dominion is wrong, for you have construed its meaning to be a subjection by force. You think of authority or control by harsh means. Your ideas are wrong – I mean, of course, in its interpretation here. Let me explain.

"Man first must recognise his own exalted status. He is the highest of sentient creation, fashioned spiritually after the similitude of the Master of the Spheres. Having realised that exalted status, man must recognise that every other living creature is also the handiwork of the same Master, and designed for the same specific reason – for the Master's own glory. Therefore, as both man and beast were designed for the same specific purpose, it follows naturally that there must be concord between the whole of created beings. You..."

"But that is a physical impossibility, Eueun," interposed Paul, argument strong within him. "Why, if upon Earth you cannot get concord between men, then how do you suppose concord is possible between man and beasts of wild nature?"

"I was speaking of original intentions, Paul – not what you find upon Earth to-day," replied Eueun gravely. "I am guiltless of dogmatising; I do not presume a knowledge of that for which I have no authority. My authority for daring to suggest what were the original intentions of the Master of the Spheres lies here in our existing economy. You find here harmony and concord between all created beings. Your life was intended to be even as ours.

"At present, as you say, it is impossible for you. Centuries of savage warfare has existed not only between man and *beast*, but between man and *man*. Yet, just as the original intention was universal harmony, so it must become an ultimate fact. For a time, Earthmen have delayed its consummation. But what we have always experienced, you must eventually experience. You dare not deny its possibility, for your ancient prophets foretell its certainty.

"And what says your poet, Tennyson? No, never mind how I know, but what says he of ultimate harmony? Listen...

> When the schemes and all the systems, kingdoms and republics fall,
> Something kindlier, higher, holier – all for each and each for all;
> All the full-brained, half-brained races, led by justice, love and truth:
> All the millions one at length with all the visions of my youth;
> All diseases quenched by science, no man halt, or deaf or blind;
> Stronger ever born of weaker, lustier body, larger mind;
> Earth at last a warless world, a single race, a single tongue.
> I have seen her far away – for is not Earth as yet so young?
> Every tiger madness muzzle, every serpent passion killed,
> Every grim ravine a garden, every blazing desert tilled,
> Robed in universal harvest up to either pole she smiles,
> Universal ocean softly, washing all her warless isles.

"So your poets, your philosophers and your prophets all visualise the ultimate harmony. What can you – what dare you say to the contrary?"

Chapter 23

It was uncanny to hear Eueun quote from our poets and explain the teaching of our ancient books. Nevertheless, his logic so fascinated me that I could not forbear a question.

"But why should such a difference exist between the conditions of Earth and Venus?" I asked him. "If, as you suggest, it was the original intention of the Master of the Spheres that harmony should exist throughout the universe, why has it proved so in your case and not in ours?"

"I cannot answer your question, Jim," replied Eueun with hesitation. "At least I could answer, but I dare not. I have already ventured beyond my allotted task, and that question you must put to Mentor. He will give you enlightenment." And there I was forced to leave the matter for a time.

Even in our conversation we had not been insensible to the glorious beauties of nature around us. It was one vast panorama of exquisite loveliness.

Presently we arrived before a magnificent rose bush, the blooms upon which were the richest and most delicate I had ever seen. We halted before its fragrant beauty and then I approached nearer to touch one of the blooms. To my amazement, I found the briar altogether devoid of thorns. Knowing the vicious prickles upon terrestrial rose bushes, I asked Eueun a cause for their absence.

"I will answer question with question," answered Eueun, smiling. "Tell me a reason for the thorns upon terrestrial rose bushes?"

"I am afraid I cannot tell you, Eueun. I know of no valid reason. All I know is that they exist." It was lamely put, I know, but truth compelled me to speak.

"Then I will tell you, Jim," said Eueun, easily. "Thorns upon terrestrial rosebushes are nature's protectors against destruction by browsing animals, and here again you are faced with your vexatious problem – disharmony and strife.

Not only war between man and man, man and beast, but strife between animals and that which the Creator willed should not be destroyed. For your animals He endowed your globe with plenty of food, and their natural food is the grass and herbs of the field. Even your carnivorous animals, according to original intentions, should be herbivorous. But..."

"That is not possible, Eueun!" I broke in upon his reasoning. "Take our terrestrial lion, for instance. He and his kind could not exist without flesh food!"

"I see," replied Eueun, musingly. "Then perhaps, Jim, you will tell me what your ancient prophet meant when he wrote 'And the lion shall eat straw like the ox'? Straw here meaning grass or hay, or, if you wish, green grass and herbs. I tell you, your own sages visualised original intentions, so why declare it to be impossible? Now, coming back to where we were. The Master of the Spheres would beautify His creation as well as provide abundant food for the creatures He has created. The rose bush is an adornment, and its essential function is to enrich and beautify. But upon your globe it cannot function without protection. Were it not for the thorns, you would possess no roses. Even under domestication, where protection is not needed against browsing animals, the thorns remain to remind you of its struggle for existence through the ages."

"It's logic, Eueun, at any rate," said Paul, with conviction. "But what I should like to know is..."

At that moment a startled cry came from Sandy. He had listened intently to Eueun's illuminating exposition, but now, as we turned to learn the reason of his cry we saw him rush to the offside of the rose bush.

"She was there!" he cried incoherently. "I saw her! Oh God! She has gone! But where? Where?"

Eueun grasped the situation in an instant, though he seemed disconcerted by its occurrence.

"Take heart, my friend," said he, compassionately, going over to the distracted man. "Just as you saw your wife a moment since, so you will see her again!"

"But why cannot I see her now, Eueun? Paul has seen her and conversed with her, and just as I see her she vanishes! It is mad'ning Eueun! Why?"

"All in good time, my dear young friend!" and we turned at an unfamiliar voice to see in our midst a man of noble bearing. It was difficult to determine his age, for though the wisdom of the ages sat upon his scholarly brow, his bright eyes and elastic step spoke of youth.

"It is Mentor!" exclaimed Eueun, joyously. "And come just at the very right time."

“Mentor!” exclaimed Sandy. “Then, sir, is it to you I look for enlightenment in this problem. Tell me of my wife, and the reason why she eludes me?”

“As I said a moment since, all in good time, my dear young friend. You all look fatigued. Shall we rest here and camp for the night?”

We were now presented in turn to Mentor, who cordially shook us each by the hand and thereby put us at our ease.

“So you have found our visitors somewhat of a handful, have you Eueun?” quoth Mentor, with sparkling eyes. “Questions rained upon you thick and fast. The ‘why’ of this, and the ‘wherefore’ of that. And you have experienced a difficulty in keeping within bounds! But Eueun, you have been the soul of discretion, and an abler interpreter I could not have sent. Thank you, lad!”

“It’s a pleasure to hear your commendation, Sir, for indeed our visitors have tried my wits to keep within bounds,” replied Eueun with a pleased smile. “Still, Mentor, there have been compensations.”

And with many a chuckle he recounted to Mentor the episode of our first night in camp.

“It was a mean trick to play upon them,” he concluded. “But, indeed, Sir, it was too good to forego.”

It was good to hear Mentor laugh. Although the laugh was against us, we did not mind, for it revealed to us that Mentor, sage though he was, could enjoy a joke.

“It must have looked funny, Eueun,” said Mentor, when his laughter had somewhat subsided.

“Funny, Sir?” replied Eueun. “Funny is scarcely the word for it. To see the three of them in a heap upon the ground, all trying desperately to disentangle themselves, then, upon separating, mixing themselves up again, was altogether too funny for words. I verily declare that old nego (the Venusian name for lion) was as much amused as I was.

Sleep came tardily to my eyes that night, but somewhat past midnight I must have fallen asleep, and it seemed but a few moments when I felt a hand placed upon my shoulder and Eueun announced breakfast.

After breakfast we continued our tramp to the city. Eueun deferentially drew back in order to let Mentor have the lead, but Mentor motioned him forward.

“You will still lead, Eueun,” said he, “and I will act as interpreter when our friends interrogate too closely.”

“Well, Mentor,” said Paul, with a smile, “it will not be long before Eueun will need your help, for we are all full to overflowing with questions. Eueun has given us answers to many questions, but there are others in which he has referred us to you. I almost fear to ask some that are in my mind, because, if I gauge the situation aright, those answers are going to be of stupendous moment. Sandy is our leader and in deference to his leadership he should advance his questions first."

"No, Paul, mine can wait for a while," answered Sandy, somewhat breathlessly. Sandy's problem was perhaps the greatest; yet, for the moment he feared to commence.

It, therefore, fell to my lot to question Mentor first. I almost hesitate to record his answers, for those answers were of the most startling character.

Chapter 24

"So you are to be the first to question me, Jim?" said Mentor after a pause. I was so glad to hear him call me by name. It put me at ease at once.

"It appears so, Sir," I answered, "although Sandy or Paul should have preceded me. But as I am to be first, I should like to put to you the question I asked of Eueun."

"And what was that, my friend?"

"It was this, Sir. Why are the conditions upon Venus so fundamentally different from those of our Earth?"

"Your use of the word 'fundamental' is correct, Jim," responded Mentor, his eyes glowing with the coming revelation. "There is a fundamental difference, and its cause you wish to know. But let us sit here awhile. We may converse better that way."

I confess with a certain amount of shame that the Bible is not a familiar book with me. But one scene of my boyhood reading came to me as we sat around

Mentor, waiting for his answer to my query. It was the scene of the Christ upon the mountainside with his disciples gathered around Him – "And He opened His mouth and taught them, saying..." etc.

Mentor sat upon a grassy knoll with the four of us reclining around him.

"You must know," he began, "that the universe is much more vast than even your advanced knowledge will give credit. It it infinite! Think for a moment of a stretch of sand somewhere upon your terrestrial seashore, and another upon our seashore here. One of you stands upon your seashore and picks up a grain of sand. Another stands upon our seashore and he also picks up a grain of sand. So small are those grains of sand that it is almost impossible to think of anything more infinitesimal without the aid of microscopic powers by which to detect their presence.

"Now let the diameter of each grain of sand represent the bounds of a solar system as vast as that of which we form a part. It is not impossible to your conception, with your knowledge of atoms, molecules and electrons. Let the distance between the two grains of sand – at present somewhere in the region of thirty millions of miles – be reckoned upon the same scale plan. And what have you? A distance so profound that your terrestrial basis of celestial measurement fails to give a name to the distance.

"Your basis of celestial measurement of distance is 'light-years', one 'light-year' representing six trillion miles. But the distance I have supposed is beyond your computation.

"We may now alter the scale plan and imagine the grains of sand to each represent, not merely the bounds of a system equal to our own, but the bounds of the distance already supposed. Then let the distance between the grains be imagined upon the new scale plan – and you then have represented one minute drop in the ocean of infinite space.

"In that infinity of space there are systems beyond the computation of moral ken, each system comprising a primary with its retinue of worlds, or planets. Not all planets are inhabited, because, in the wisdom of the Master of the Spheres, planetary generation and regeneration is constantly and eternally taking place. But every system contains, within its bounds, the principle of actual or potential habitability. Myriads of systems contain sentient life, but – here is the first step to the solution of your problem – no other system contains within its bounds what is contained within ours. I whisper the word, and it is: disharmony.

"How that disharmony originated I must leave for another time. Sufficient for me now to say is that this system of ours has passed through two cataclysmic periods – premature disintegration – in order to try and exterminate the germ of disharmony. But even the fierce heat of incandescence failed to entirely eradicate it. Originally it pervaded the system.

"In the regeneration of the system, the germ became active in two planets only. In the second regeneration it became active only in one – your planet, Terra. Now comes the most beautiful topic which sentient lips can speak, the sublimest thought which sentient minds can conceive. The Master of the Spheres willed not again to regenerate the system by premature disintegration, but He willed to regenerate by plunging your world into the abyss of His infinite Love! Such a declaration could have but one interpretation – regeneration by redemption! If the germ of disharmony survived the heat of incandescent disintegration, then it was truly formidable. But its formidable character could be neutralised and changed by absorption in redemptive Love.

"My friends, although we of this planet do not participate in Redemption, we thrill at its stupendous nature. None but the mind of Deity could conceive of such a plan, and none but Omnipotence could bring it to fruition.

"But see what such a process involves! It involves a wonder of such magnitude that the problem of infinite space or infinite time falls by comparison into insignificance. The germ seed of disharmony progressed by inheritance throughout the entire terrestrial race. No single being upon your Earth could possibly be exempt. It lay active at the very core of your constitution, and the soil in which it lay was congenial to its continued malignant progress.

"How then could it be checked? Not in the crucible of incandescent disintegration, as I have already shown, but in the awful necessity of absorption by the Deity. The Heir to the Spheres would absorb within Himself the seed germ in order to neutralise its power, purify its purpose and redirect its energies. To use a phrase out of your sacred records: "He who knew no sin became sin that He may redeem those who were in sin." That phrase really means that the Heir absorbed the germ seed of disharmony within Himself in order that He may bring beauty and concord to a disharmonious world.

"May I simplify what I have been trying to say to you by quoting a parable out of your sacred records?

"A man has a hundred sheep, and at counting time, one is discovered missing. Only one is lost, my friends, yet the owner is troubled. No rest can he enjoy until he has found that one; over mountain and hill, through thicket and swamp, counting no cost too heavy until at last he finds it. Upon his shoulders he lays the weary sheep, returning home with rejoicing. His flock is once more complete, for he has found the lost one and restored it to the fold.

"One world is lost to harmony out of the myriads which constitute the Universe. By the sublime Redemptive work of the Heir to the Spheres, the key to harmony is supplied. But such is the magnanimity of the Master of the Spheres, the key is not forced but offered. He who has the power to compel allegiance wills rather to impel allegiance by Love.

"Gradually but surely, disharmony will be eliminated from your globe. It will be eliminated by the consent and the wish of its inhabitants. The time has been long in coming to fruition, but come it will. Then throughout the Universe will ring the glad anthem of complete restoration, of complete harmony. That, my dear young friends, is the reason for the fundamental difference between this planet and your own."

For a long time after Mentor had ceased speaking, there was complete silence. That which he had imparted to us was of too momentous a character to comment upon before fully assimilating its import. Therefore we remained mute before its profundity.

Chapter 25

As we continued to ponder over the momentous things told us by Mentor, he arose from his sitting posture upon the knoll.

"Come along my friends," said he at last, "too much thought in one day will not be good for you. Let us continue our journey to the city. You will find relaxation there, and we can continue our conversation later."

Personally I was not sorry for the suggestion. The more I thought, the more confused became my mind. There were so many questions I wanted to ask that I could scarcely arrange them in order. I could see that Sandy and Paul were similarly placed.

As we reached the outskirts, we entered one of the spacious playing fields which entirely surrounded the city. In the one we entered there were scores of children at play, and one would have had little difficulty in thinking one was upon our own Earth, witnessing English children at their games. Yet in some indescribable way there was a difference. I tried to probe wherein the difference lay, but the solution was elusive. I whispered my problem to Sandy, who was standing a little apart from the rest.

"Yes, Jim," answered Sandy in a low tone. "I also detected there existed a difference, and have been puzzling for a solution. But I think I have it now. I can best describe it by saying it lies in the glory of perfect physical health, spiritual beauty, and in the absolute freedom from restraint."

I caught the gleam of Sandy's meaning, and as I watched I saw that he could scarcely have given a better explanation. Boys and girls played their games in concert, the smaller children in their own particular groups and the elder in similar groups. Throughout the playing fields no weakling stood aloof, afraid to join in the fun through fear of hurt. Their faces were lit with the beauteous light of carefree joy. There was an entire absence of curiosity or embarrassment.

Then occurred a scene I shall not readily forget.

The river which we had more or less followed in our journey to the city ran through the children's playing field. It escaped the city by a sharp bend to the right. There was no manner of protection along its banks, and it occurred to me to be rather dangerous for young children. Sandy and I were still conversing when we heard a startled cry from Paul.

"Heaven, boys," he cried. "There's a little one gone over the bank."

Paul was an excellent sprinter, and away he raced to the rescue. Not one article of clothing did he divest himself of. For a second he stood poised, then disappeared into the water. As we reached the bank we saw with a sigh of relief he needed no help from us. He had grasped the child and was now within a yard or so of the bank. Tenderly Sandy reached down for the little dripping child and safely deposited her upon the bank. To our surprise she gave a gay young laugh and scampered off, apparently little the worse for her adventure. We saw her join the group of her companions and went on playing as though nothing untoward had happened to her.

"Paul," said Mentor, going over to his side. "Let me shake you by the hand. It was a noble impulse which prompted you to do what you have just done, and one that particularly commended itself to me. It was an impulse to help one whom you believed to be weak and in danger; an impulse to save. You know me now to be your friend, and I would say naught to detract from the high merit of your deed. Yet my dear young friend, I must tell you there was no need for it. You..."

"But Mentor, the little one would have drowned had Paul not dived in," remonstrated Sandy, aghast that Mentor should suggest the needlessness of Paul's action.

"What Mentor says is true, Sandy," said Eueun, who had hitherto been a silent watcher of events. "I quite agree with Mentor as to the nobility of the impulse, and nothing can detract from its merits. At the same time, strange as it may seem to you, I must also agree that the act was needless. May I show them, Sir? Thank you. Here, Tesea! Come to me, little one. Now jump into the river."

A little maid of about four toddled up to Eueun with her face beaming with laughter. Without the least hesitation she sprang into the river. Like a cork she floated upon the surface of the stream, then, turning round, she gently paddled with her little hands to the bank. A dip in the bank enabled her to ascend without the least assistance, and with a wave of her hands she ran to rejoin her companions in their games.

"But, Mentor, the little one will catch cold," Paul expostulated, the medical instinct alive within him. "Both the one I rescued and this little one ought to have a change of clothing and a rub down at once!"

"And what of yourself, Paul?" asked Mentor smilingly. "You also have been in the river."

"Why, yes," said Paul. And then he paused. "Well, that's strange. I feel not the slightest discomfort. In fact, no one would believe I had been in the river. Even my clothing is dry! How do you account for this Mentor?"

"One thing at a time Paul," responded Mentor. "It will take you many months to fully realise the tremendous difference between the planet from which you have come and that upon which you now are. You and your friends, because of Earth experiences, will be making mistakes with constant persistency. You will see, day by day, folk whom to your eyes will be in positions of danger. And through it all will be the impulse to help and assist. But it is all needless, my friends! Did not Eueun tell you in the early stages of your visit that pain, suffering, sorrow and death were things unknown to the native population of this planet? And because these things are unknown, it must of necessity follow that danger is also unknown. The little one who fell in the river was, to you, in a position of danger, either of drowning or of a subsequent cold or chill. But to Eueun and I, she was in danger of neither, because indisposition and death are unknown here."

"But this is little short of the miraculous!" protested Sandy.

"That is where you are wrong, Sandy, when you use the word 'miraculous'," said Mentor, with a patient smile. "By using that word, you suggest these things to be abnormal. They are not *abnormal*, my dear young friend, but *normal*. It is Earth life which is abnormal, not the life we live here. Our conditions are consistent with the original intentions of the Master of the Spheres. Your conditions are its antithesis. And the cause of your condition is the presence of the seed germ of disharmony.

"But do not despair. There are heroisms being performed day by day upon your globe which are purifying your life universal and, gradually but surely, are leading up to the fulfilment of original intentions. The Heir to the Spheres has shown the possibility of living the life of perfect harmony; a life of perfect concord. The pity is that your fellow beings are so slow to realise its possibility.

"When finally it does mature, and the whole of terrestrial beings are living in perfect amity and concord, the wonder will be why previous generations delayed the joys of its consummation. But come along, we can converse as we walk. There are so many things I am anxious to show you. I think too, you will probably understand better if you see things, rather than merely have them told to you."

As we walked along, Mentor told us we were to receive hospitality at a house close to the college over which he presided. With joy we heard that Eueun was to remain with us during our stay.

Chapter 26

The days which followed our entry into the city were days of wonderful and stimulating interest. No day passed but that some item was added to our accumulating knowledge.

We found, even as Mentor had stated, that every feature connected with sickness and suffering was conspicuous by its entire absence. Hospitals, surgeries, dispensaries, convalescent homes, chemists shops and drug stores, with all their ramifications and extensions, were non-existent. So, too, with law. Courts of Justice, penal establishments, houses of detention, reformatories, rescue homes, mental institutes, were all unknown. There were no Poor Law institutions.

In regard to the former, Paul, the medical man of our party, wished to know how the people kept fit.

"There is nothing strange in that," replied Mentor. "First and foremost there is no predisposition to ailment by transmission. Every child born is perfect in health, even before it draws its first, separate breath. Fresh air, exercise and natural sustenance, with perfect contentment, continues to keep every individual being in perfect health throughout its subsequent life."

But the medico would not be denied. Granted perfect health for a sustained period, what of the end? Was there no diminishing of powers, of strength, of perception? In fact, what was the end of Venusian individual life?

"Look at me, Paul," replied Mentor with a smile. "I have lived 80 Venusian years, which is a period approximating to 53 of your terrestrial years. I shall continue to live here until I reach an age equal to 100 of your terrestrial years.

"My age then, according to the Venusian periods, will be 150 years. Yet at that time my energies will be unimpaired. My sight, hearing and all my faculties will be as clear and keen as they are now, and as they were at 30 or 20 years of age. There will be no flagging of my steps and no falter in my voice."

"And what then?" asked Paul, who had followed Mentor with breathless interest.

"Having accomplished my work here, I shall simply be removed to another sphere of activity!" replied Mentor quietly.

"To where?" asked Sandy.

"That is a matter with which I never concern myself," Mentor made answer. "All that I know is that the sphere of activity will be of a higher order than this, and that I shall be one step nearer to the effulgent glory where dwells the Master of the Spheres."

But our days were not all spent in probing into recondite problems. We had relaxations of lighter texture. One episode in particular I would record. It was none other than our attendance at a Venusian wedding.

All suggestion of grossness is absent from the mating of a man and maid. Wooing is a natural gravitation of two kindred souls, and the subsequent marriage is the ideal of a perfect merging of the twain into one.

Eueun acted as a friend and guide to our little party. With something of embarrassment we found ourselves to be as important as many of the guests present. Everyone was kind to us and we were interested spectators of all that took place.

The bride was an exquisite figure of her perfect girlhood, her native charms intensified by her attire of silvery whiteness. No less imposing was the bridegroom, standing as he did just under six feet tall, broad of shoulder and strong of limb.

Bride and bridegroom walked to the church, arriving simultaneously. In the vestibule they stood a moment together and then parted, the bride traversing the right hand aisle alone.

At the lower end of the aisles, bride and groom halted and faced each other. At that moment the priest (as we should term him) advanced from the altar with hands outstretched, and beckoned the two towards him. Slowly they advanced and met in front of him. Taking their two hands, he clasped them together.

As they joined hands, the great organ pealed forth a paean of joyous music, and the vast congregation, rising to their feet, filled the edifice with melodious singing.

It was all delightfully simple. No oral vows, glibly spoken and quickly forgotten. The only ritual attending the ceremony was each walking an individual path towards the altar – emphasising the fact that up to that moment they were individually separate, and joined by the priest at the altar thereby emphasising that now they were one. Simplicity, devotion and reverence were stamped upon every phase of that short and effective service.

The scene which followed was one with which we were more or less familiar. Gaiety and laughter held sway, and the fun was delightfully exhilarating. Paul danced exquisitely, and soon he was quite at home with a Venusian maid upon his arm.

No amount of inducement would make Sandy take the floor, although he could dance with consummate skill. Memory was strong within him at that moment, and he stood watching the gay throng with a sad, pensive expression.

Suddenly I heard Eueun's laughing voice. "Come along, Jim! Here is Myso, waiting to be introduced."

"No, Miss Myso," said I, in answer to her smiling invitation. "I've never danced a step in my life."

"What did you call me?" asked she with a mystified air.

"Myso is mystified at your mode of address," Eueun said, with an amused smile. "You must drop all prefixes here, Jim. Everyone is known by name, whether man, maid or matron." So with some hesitation on my part, it had to be Myso.

I found Myso a very companionable girl, and soon we were conversing like old friends. Although she knew that Sandy, Paul and I were from Terra, her whole attitude was devoid of the slightest curiosity. In fact, this remarkable feature was evidenced throughout our stay upon the planet. Not one question was asked us of our life upon Terra, other than by Mentor – although every endeavour was made to show us every feature of their own economy.

"Now Myso," said I to my companion, during a lull in the gaiety, "I want to get old Sandy interested. Have you got such a thing as a guitar? If so, I am going to get Paul to sing to you, with Sandy as accompanist."

Myso soon produced a guitar, and Sandy came out of his reverie when he had his beloved instrument in his hand. To my surprise, Paul proved somewhat difficult. He certainly never suffered much from embarrassment, yet he was reluctant to sing.

"No, old man," he whispered to me, when I approached him. "I'd rather not sing just now. As a matter of fact, Merna was just going to show me the gardens." (Merna was the young lady with whom Paul had been dancing.)

I looked at Paul, somewhat startled. I knew of his impetuous nature but, like me, he was good and true. Despite this, he was of course only human, with the red blood of manhood flowing through his veins. I had heard him say, many times, in his jocular way, "Why a mild flirtation is the salt of life."

At any rate, up to this moment no woman had ever seriously touched his heart. Had he now lost his head and felt he was in love with a Venusian maid? Surely such a thing was preposterous! Mentor would never permit such a thing – and I turned from Paul, greatly perturbed.

Chapter 27

Paul evidently realised I had turned from him in a disturbed frame of mind, for he came to me quickly: "Sorry, old man," said he, hastily. "Of course, I will sing. Merna will show me the gardens later."

I was glad and infinitely relieved to hear him speak so. But had I known what the outcome of his associations with Merna would be, I should not have been so easy in my mind. It led to a premature abandonment of our stay upon Venus, and a forced return to the old Earth. But that regrettable episode I must not anticipate.

Paul sang that day with supreme elation. It was a wild Arab love song, foreign to the audience both in its tempestuous presentation, and in its subtle morality. Personally I doubted its wisdom, but the audience stood or sat, entranced. When Paul had concluded, Merna hastened towards him, but Eueun interposed with a strange look upon his face.

"It was sung beautifully, Paul," said Eueun, with genuine frankness. "But if you sing again, change the character of the song, there's a good fellow. No, it is perhaps that you do not know, but no wooing of that character occurs here."

Paul sang one more song. This time he satisfied Eueun's desire, for Eueun was as vociferous in his applause as any of the audience. We all voted our relaxation an entire success. Previous to the breaking-up of the party, Merna took Paul with her upon an excursion round the gardens. The impetuous excitability of his nature was noticeable to me upon his return, but I trusted no untoward incident would occur to mar our stay upon the planet Venus.

That night we had a recurrence of the weird and distressing circumstances which attended our last few hours in the machine. This time we had the presence of Eueun, yet the episode completely unnerved us for a time.

Eueun and I shared a room, Paul being on one side of us, alone, and Sandy on the other side, alone. Separating for the night, we could presently hear Sandy softly playing the guitar, which he had begged leave to borrow for the night.

"Sandy's living in the past to-night, Eueun," said I, with deep feelings of sympathy going out to my old chum and chief. "Accompanying Paul in his songs has intensified memory, rather than allayed it."

"Yes," answered Eueun, in what I thought to be a very contemplative mood. Then he said abruptly, "You can turn in Jim! I think I'll sit and read for a while."

There was something in Eueun's tones that caused all desire for sleep to vanish. His attitude was suggestive of waiting and watching. What it portended I could not define, but it caused me to say that I, too, would remain up and add a few more notes towards the narrative I intended to write of our adventures.

"So you intend to publish the record of your adventures when you return to the Earth?" queried Eueun, with a smile.

"Why, certainly," I replied.

"And what will the folk say who read it, Jim? Will they think it true?"

To the casual observer, Eueun was interested in the inquiry. But I knew he was tense and waiting for something to happen. Still, I would not betray my thoughts, or let Eueun see I had detected his preoccupation. I therefore answered him thus: "Well, as to that, Eueun. I do no think I concern myself overmuch."

"No, perhaps it is just as well you do not worry yourself over its anticipated reception," said Eueun, quietly. "I'll tell you now what your folk will say. They will say it is twaddle and nonsense, and that it is inconsistent with every elementary truth. That which you have been able to achieve, the knowledge you have gained, will be yours and your companions', alone. No one else will believe a single word you write. And you will not be able to lay blame upon them for their disbelief. It is altogether contradictory to what they have been taught. It will take years to..."

Eueun paused. There was profound silence.

Then faintly there came the sound of Sandy's guitar. He was playing the melody which Paul sang when on the voyage to Venus, the song which led Sandy to tell us of the tragedy in his life.

Suddenly the melody ceased. In its stead there came the sound of a terrific struggle. The transition from melody to strife came with appalling abruptness.

No sooner was the sound heard than Eueun was upon his feet. With "Stay where you are, Jim!" he was gone.

Imperious as was his command, I could do no other but follow. I was at the threshold of Sandy's room as quickly as was Eueun. Wild-eyed and panting, Sandy was struggling with an invisible assailant. I knew that at once. It was a repetition of the scene which followed the removal of the man-tunnel cover of our machine. To and fro across the room he staggered, the veins upon his forehead protruding like knotted cords.

"Desist!" cried Eueun authoritatively, striding into the room. But no cessation came to the struggle.

"In the name of the Master of the Spheres, desist!" cried Eueun again.

Like a stone projected from a catapult, Sandy was released and fell across the bed as though he was no more. Eueun paid no attention to Sandy, but stood with stern, set face, looking apparently at the far corner of the room. What he saw was unseen by me. Yet though invisible to me, I realised it was very real and tangible to Eueun. With stern, uncompromising language, he spoke.

"What is the meaning of this attack upon my guest?" demanded Eueun, with ill-suppressed indignation. "Once before thou didst retard thy progress by wilful and malignant wrongdoing. Hast thou not learnt the wisdom from that which befell thee the last time thou didst commit wrong? Get thee hence! And in the name of the Heir to the Spheres, who has done so much for thee, beware lest thou art sent to the outer darkness for an aeon. Begone!"

Whatever influence for evil had been present, I realised by Eueun's relaxed tension it had vanished. With a sigh of relief I turned to Sandy, but found to my consternation he had not regained consciousness.

"Eueun!" I cried, in the agony of my feelings, "Old Sandy is not dead, surely? Come quickly, for the love of heaven, and do what you can for him!"

"It is nothing to worry about, Jim," said Eueun kindly. "Let him rest so for a little while. It is the shock more than any physical hurt that has rendered him unconscious. Let him come to, gradually. He'll be quite normal when he awakes. I'll call Paul, so that you two can be with him. Now, do not worry, Jim. You can depend upon my word. Sandy will be himself again in a very short while."

With that, Eueun left me, and I sat by the side of the bed, waiting for my old comrade to recover.

What was this strange, inexplicable something which had attacked Sandy on two occasions? Eueun had said that pain, suffering and disharmony were unknown on Venus, and Mentor had confirmed and emphasised this statement. Yet here upon the bed, Sandy was slowly recovering from an attack by some evil influence. And this influence was here in the constitution of Venus!

What was meant by this contradiction?

But, stay! Was there contradiction? I remembered now. Both Eueun and Mentor had qualified that statement by adding that only the inhabitants, native to the planet, were immune from sickness, death and disharmony! Were there other beings living upon this planet who were not native Venusians?

These thoughts ran through my mind as I watched by the bed. So I continued to ponder, when Eueun returned to the room.

"Jim," said Eueun quietly, "Paul is not in his room."

"Not in his room?" I echoed vaguely.

"No!" replied Eueun. "In fact, I think he has left the house."

Chapter 28

The fact that Paul was not in the house filled me with a vague alarm. Where could he have gone, and for what purpose? I glanced at Eueun, but his face was inscrutable.

At that moment, a step was heard upon the stairs. Eueun went quietly out of the room, returning in a moment with Paul.

"Good heavens! Jim! What has happened to Sandy?"

Before I could answer, Sandy roused.

"It is all right, old man," said I, in answer to Sandy's look of bewilderment. You are with Eueun, Paul and I. Lie down and sleep. There's no need for apprehension!"

Sandy took me at my word and, with a tired smile, relaxed upon the bed. In a moment or two, he was fast asleep.

"Eueun," said I, turning to him, "you expected something of this sort to happen, did you not?"

"What makes you think that, Jim?" queried Eueun, in a manner that suggested an attempt at evasion.

"Your general attitude," I answered. "We were conversing, but your attention was elsewhere. You were tense with expectation: so much so that I knew something was amiss. But tell me the meaning of it all, there's a good fellow. I am more than ever in the dark over this matter and would wish to know its meaning."

"I expected you would be full of questionings, Jim," responded Eueun. "But let it rest for a time. Presently you will know all, and through a source you little expect. Let us leave Sandy now, for he has another experience coming to him in which we cannot share. So let us retire to our rooms and get what sleep we can, to-morrow may be a somewhat heavy day for you."

There was something in Eueun's tone which forbade me questioning him further. Also, within my breast there was a vague apprehension of disaster. What its cause could be, I could not well define. But I was conscious that some barrier had arisen which threatened our further stay upon the planet.

Whether Paul felt the same, I could not say. He uttered not a word, but turned and went to his room. Eueun and I followed to our room, but my subsequent sleep was exceedingly troubled.

The following morning I made a hasty toilet and proceeded downstairs in order to indulge in a stroll before breakfast. I waited for a moment, thinking Paul or Sandy might have joined me, but as neither put in an appearance, I ventured out alone. I had proceeded scarcely a hundred yards when I ran into Mentor.

"Well, Jim," said he, with a quiet intonation, "you are astir early. I am glad you are alone, for there are one or two things I wish to say to you. First and foremost, you must inform your companions that an almost immediate return to the Earth is desirable. In fact, not only desirable, but necessary."

"What in heaven's name is the matter, Sir?" I exclaimed, aghast at the confirmation of my fears. It was horrible to think of a return to the Earth when our adventures were but beginning.

"The cause for the moment may be left on one side," said Mentor, with quiet emphasis. "Sufficient for me to say that something has occurred which necessitates your immediate return. The circumstances are these... But listen!

Come here with me!" And Mentor pulled me hastily behind a shrub growing in a garden, close at hand.

I listened with bated breath. I could now detect the sound of approaching footsteps. Slowly the steps came abreast of where we were concealed. To my surprise – but apparently not to the surprise of Mentor – it was Paul and Merna.

As I glanced through the shrub, I saw that every evidence pointed to the fact that Paul had not retired to rest at all. He had probably slipped out of the house again when Eueun and I went to our room after leaving Sandy.

"I have done you an injury, Merna, darling," I heard Paul say, as they were passing us. "But forgive me! I will see Mentor presently. I think there would be nothing in the way of my remaining here and making you my wife."

What Merna's answer was to Paul's suggestion I do not know, for by this time they had passed out of hearing.

"Come along, Jim," said Mentor gently. "We will walk a little this way and then return to breakfast."

"Just a moment, sir!" said I, and for an instant I felt so shaken I thought I was about to faint. "Is what we have just witnessed the cause of our return? Is it because of Paul and Merna?"

"Yes, Jim," responded Mentor slowly, "it is because of Paul and Merna."

"But surely, Mentor, there are other ways out of the difficulty beside that of our return to the Earth?" I pleaded. "Paul could be persuaded from seeing Merna. I suppose that... that marriage is..."

"Quite out of the question!" said Mentor decidedly. "Marriage between Paul and Merna would not merely be impolitic, it would be... No, it is utterly impossible! In regard to persuading Paul not to see Merna, that now is futile. The harm has been done and both must pay the price."

"But great heavens! Mentor, what harm has been done?" I exclaimed somewhat heatedly, stung to the defence of Paul. "Paul would not compromise the honour of Merna! I know he is impetuous, but..."

"You do not understand the circumstances, Jim," said Mentor, in no way abashed at my vehement defence of Paul. "I shall, of course, see Paul. But at the same time, whatever the outcome of the interview, you must make every endeavour to leave Venus. That is imperative!"

"But, sir, our task has scarcely commenced!" I protested vigorously. "Surely one human slip ought not to be of sufficient importance to warrant the cessation of our enterprise."

"So argue all of earthly origin," replied Mentor patiently. "And so will argue Paul and Merna."

"Merna?" I queried wonderingly. "But Merna is not of earthly origin."

"I told you a moment ago you did not understand, lad." And Mentor's voice had perceptibly risen. "Merna is of earthly origin and therein lies the tragedy. But I see I must make this clear to you.

"You must understand that upon Venus there are two distinct classes of individuals living. First, there are those who are native to the planet. As you have previously been told, those born here are free of all predisposition to ailments. Also they are born free of all disposition to wrongdoing.

"Each child therefore starts life with hereditary tendencies to virtue. So positive is this strain that young children are instinctively virtuous.

"The period of instinctive virtue lasts for eight years. At eight years of age each child acts upon his or her own responsibility. That is to say, instinctive actions become acts of volition. You will appreciate that transition is easy, seeing that life here in all its ramifications is pure.

"But there are others living upon Venus. These know of a different life from our life – a life in which sin, sorrow and death have part.

"Yes, lad, I can see you know now who they are. They are those who come from your Earth, after passing through the gateway of physical death. Venus is the second stage in the development of their spiritual character. Both the good and the evil come here. The good materialise quickly, and upon the full establishment of their virtue, join in our life here. After a period, satisfactory to themselves, they pass on to the third stage of their development.

"In regard to the evil, these we encourage to a life of virtue. It is a task needing the utmost patience. Sometimes a long period elapses before improvement is shown. But sooner or later all show signs of development, and when a certain stage of improvement is reached they also materialise."

Mentor paused for a moment in his recital of these wonderful facts. I had followed him with breathless interest. But during the pause, I could not forbear to ask a question.

"How does this affect Merna?"

Chapter 29

"How does it affect Merna?" queried Mentor, echoing the question I had put to him. "It affects her very greatly indeed!

"Merna's life upon Earth was lived upon an exceeding low plane. Desire ruled her life to such an extent that she was but 35 years of age when she came here. For a long time, earthly memory held her in bondage, but eventually she began a development towards the higher life. One short year ago, she reached the stage of complete materialisation, and I thought her safe. Now it is as though her development had never been. Her pilgrimage must be traversed again.

No physical harm or hurt can devolve upon Merna, because she is not physical in the sense that you understand. It is moral harm that has happened to her.

Through her associations with Paul, earthly memories have been revived and her status is thereby lowered. Merna is even now invisible to Paul! It is a great pity, and the only redeeming feature is that Merna can and will rise again to the exalted state she enjoyed but a few short hours ago. But let us return. Eueun will have breakfast ready by now."

As we retraced our steps, my heart beat fast with indignation against Paul. Mentor must have sensed my feelings, and with that wonderful intuition he possessed was able to detect the true cause of my indignation.

"Your indignation is unworthy of you, Jim," he chided, gently. "You are angry with Paul, not because he has harmed Merna, but because his action has curtailed your visit here. Such thoughts are selfish and certainly do you no credit. Be sorry for Paul, not angry with him. And in your prayers remember, with compassion, Merna. In all your subsequent life, never broach this subject to Paul. Presently he will give you the details of his own accord. And remember this, lad: his own condemnation will be his punishment."

I felt too ashamed to speak. Mentor had rightly divined my thoughts. We proceeded for a while in silence. Then, with a smile, Mentor turned to me.

"There is a question you wish to ask, is there not, my boy?"

"You must be a perfect wizard, Mentor," I replied, startled out of my reverie. "Yes, there is a question agitating my mind and it is this: you said that Merna could and would rise again to the exalted state which was her's before she met Paul. Is this true in all cases? Why I ask is because our theologians upon Earth teach a doctrine which seems to me to be devilish rather than divine. They teach of a Hell – a place of perpetual anguish and torture. And they say if folk upon Earth die unrepentant, they go to this place of perpetual torment. Yet, from what you have told me, it seems to me, Merna died unrepentant. Can you explain this?"

"Oh, Jim!" said Mentor, with more vigour than I had yet heard him speak. "If only your theologians knew the harm they are doing in teaching this pernicious doctrine, they would cease this very instant to propagate it. No doctrine belies the nature and character of the Master of the Spheres as this. To teach it is to insult Him. It is preposterous, cruel, and, as you stated a moment ago, devilish.

"And your theologians are not consistent. They teach that the design of punishment is reclaimative [ie, restorative]. Yet, in the same breath, they claim it to be destructive. How is it possible to reclaim if every avenue of reclamation is closed? Such teaching has the logic of a child whose mind is undeveloped.

"It ranks on a par with the action of your so-called civilised countries. I mean, those countries wherein capital punishment takes place. If it was not for the pitiful tragedy involved, it would be the most amusing thing upon your Earth. Remember, Jim, the design of punishment is to reclaim! But how can you hope to reclaim human beings by killing them? It is the height of absurdity!

"No, lad, I'll not beat about the bush over this matter. No human being is banished to perpetual exile. The period of their exile from joy and happiness is contingent upon their efforts to develop the higher and nobler faculties. And every human being has the same chance of recovery. Believe me, Jim, there is no deception and no flaw in that which is controlled by the Master of the Spheres."

"Do those who pass over begin with any degree of advantage?" I asked. "I mean, of course, those who die unrepentant."

"Not one whit!" replied Mentor with emphasis. And then he added, slowly, "Except the advantage of naked realisation."

I am afraid I did not quite see what Mentor meant by his extension, and frankly told him so.

"When terrestrial beings die, their real status accompanies them here," continued Mentor. "It matters not a jot what they were supposed to be on Earth. Their souls are here stripped bare, and we know them for what they are. They may deceive their fellows all through their adult life. Here no deception is possible. They stand before us as they really and truly are. Let me quote you an example.

"Sandy, as you know, has been attacked on two occasions by a malignant influence. I term it an 'influence' because it is invisible to you. But I know it to be the spirit of a man who has passed over from your Earth. So evil is he that as long as he remains in his present state, it is utterly impossible for him to materialise. He must therefore remain so until, of his own volition, he seeks the higher life.

"That man on Earth was believed to be a paragon of virtue. His companionship was sought by all shades of society. He was goodness personified to human eyes. At his death, thousands went into genuine mourning. The newspapers eulogised his supposed virtues, and a large, publicly subscribed monument marks the place of his moral remains.

"But here he was stripped of all his sham and pretence. He stood revealed in all his naked ugliness. He was consigned to my ministrations in order to assist him to the higher life. But just as he was mean and selfish and unrepentant upon Earth, so did I find him here.

"Craftily and with perfect ease, he had murdered an elder brother in order to possess a great inheritance. The sweet girl who was his brother's betrothed nearly became insane. By Satan's own cunning, he wooed her and eventually married her. She, out of all the people who were his companions and friends, knew his real character. Evil as she knew him to be, her loyalty would not permit her to denounce him.

"Patiently I dealt with him that he may be repentant of his many sins. But just as he was of flint in his life upon Earth, so was he here. He cursed me when I tried to lead him to higher thoughts and, up to the present, has proved altogether unapproachable.

"When your party arrived here, he saw in the pure love of Sandy for his dearly departed wife, the antithesis of his own unnatural cravings. With devilish cunning, he set about a plan to paralyse the spirit of Sandy in order that his own unclean spirit may occupy Sandy's body. Then he intended to appear before Sandy's wife (who has materialised long since) and attempt her downfall. But all his efforts have been frustrated, and your leader will have a wonderful story to tell on the voyage back to the Earth."

While Mentor had been imparting to me this wonderful narrative relating to the after life of terrestrial beings, I had lost all count of time. But now I woke up to the realisation that Eueun and the rest would be anxious at my absence. Mentor took my arm and, with a smile, hurried me along towards the house.

"Now mind, Jim," he cautioned, "not a word to Paul or Sandy."

When we arrived, there were several things which caught my attention. For all Paul's expressions of contrition when he passed Mentor and I, he was now in a boisterous mood, gay and irresponsible.

And I saw too, that though Eueun answered him apparently in the same gay way, a profound gravity rested upon his noble eyes. Sandy was not yet down.

"Come along, Jim," said Eueun, hastily. "Now you and Mentor are come, we'll have breakfast."

"Are we not going to wait for old stick-in-the-mud?" Paul asked, gaily.

"No," responded Eueun quietly. "We'll carry on. Sandy will be here in a few moments."

As Eueun intimated, it was but a few moments before the door opened and Sandy came in. And what a change. I expected to see him pale and drawn through the terrible experience he had but lately encountered. But no! Sandy was radiantly transformed. His face shone as though it reflected the glory of some angelic presence. His every glance and act suggested gold that had been purged of all dross through purifying fires.

As he took Mentor's hand with his right, and Eueun's with his left hand, I could see there was perfect understanding between them. Then turning to us, he said: "Boys, we must make all ready to-night, for we leave Venus to-morrow!"

There was no regret in Sandy's voice. But rather a deep, vibrant joy, was expressed therein. Not so Paul. He sprang to his feet with blazing eyes of protest.

Chapter 30

That Sandy should announce our early return to the Earth was altogether inexplicable to me. How could he have known? Eueun could have said nothing to him, seeing that Sandy had been left entirely undisturbed after his period of unconsciousness. I knew, too, that Mentor had not seen him for hours previous to the attack upon him.

And yet Sandy knew!

The strange part about it was that he expressed no sorrow at our early departure from Venus. Rather, there appeared a deep peace upon him. It was as though he had been transported into the seventh heaven of delight, with the glow and the glory still upon him. His knowledge, therefore, and his present condition, was a problem altogether beyond me.

The announcement of our early departure had a tumultuous effect upon Paul. He sprang to his feet with a violent gesture, and with eyes blazing with indignation.

"Leave Venus to-morrow?" he cried. "Why, man alive! That is altogether impossible! We have been here but a few days, and we calculated upon staying a year at least. We have seen comparatively nothing of the planet as yet. What put such an idea into your head, man?"

Sandy had ever been patient with both Paul and I. But now a gentle compassion mingled with and glorified his patience.

"Paul, old man," said he gently, "I know we have seen but little of the planet; nothing to what we had hoped. Nevertheless it is imperative that we leave Venus.

"Old friend, if you did but know, there is a far greater inducement for me to remain than for you. Believe me, there is a sense in which it will be exceedingly hard for me to return to the Earth. But we must go, Paul! We must start tomorrow!"

Whether Sandy knew the real reason for our curtailed visit, I had no knowledge. If he did, he certainly did not betray the fact, either by look or gesture. Not one word of reproach did he utter to Paul. Only a great yearning tenderness towards his old companion and friend.

"But we will not leave Venus!" exclaimed Paul, with passion. "Good God, man! How can I leave? Merna – I love her; love her as I never thought it possible for a human being to love! Merna!"

As Paul called his beloved's name, his passion became spent. Brokenly, he turned to Mentor.

"I was coming to see you this morning, Mentor, to ask consent that I may woo Merna. I have no wish to return to the Earth. I ask no greater joy, but to remain here as the husband of her whom I love. Oh, how I love her, Sir! Every fibre of my being thrills to call her mine! Will... will you not give consent?"

"You ask an impossible thing, my young friend," replied Mentor gently. "I will not hurt you by saying your proposal is preposterous, seeing you are altogether ignorant of what you ask. But believe me, Paul, even had Merna been a true Venusian, such an alliance would not be permitted. Seeing she is what she is... the question is not one of permission – but one of utter impossibility."

"But it is yourself, Mentor, who does not understand," said Paul, with desperate intensity. "I... I... Heavens, no! I cannot explain. I..."

Paul broke off, helpless and inarticulate. Down went his head. I turned away that I should not witness his agony. Yet even as I turned away, I could not but help seeing his face flushed with a scarlet hue. I guessed its significance – it was a flush of shame.

"Paul!" called Mentor, with startling directness. "I had intended you should depart from Venus without again seeing Merna. Our conversation, however, has decided me otherwise. No explanation upon my part will make you see wisdom. This evening you shall see Merna again. You shall see her alone. Merna will explain, and though that explanation will not be as you expect, you will at least understand clearly.

"But, good friends all, let us breakfast! I will join you. Eueun, serve up, lad, for I am hungry. One word more: let us all forget our recent conversation and enjoy breakfast."

I was intensely grateful to Mentor for his magnanimity towards Paul. It certainly put new life into our old comrade, and we sat down to a breakfast of Eueun's preparation with a satisfactory appetite. No reference was made to our recent conversation. I knew that our departure was inevitable, and I bowed my head to its finality.

After breakfast, Eueun enquired from Mentor the programme for the day, to which he replied he would like us to visit one of the places of industry, a few miles from the city. Much as I should like this, I felt the greater need was to visit our machine to see that all was in readiness for our return journey to the Earth. Not wishing to hurt Paul, I took Eueun aside and mentioned this to him.

"Don't worry about that, Jim," answered Eueun quietly. "You will find that all details have been attended to. The oxygen tanks will be recharged, and your store of concentrated food will be inspected and replenished. You have nothing to do but enjoy the last few remaining hours."

"It is such an infinite pity, Eueun," I began, but Eueun prevented me further with a sudden gesture.

"Don't, Jim!" said he. And I was surprised to find his tones, which I can only express as near to tears. But as this expression of emotion was unknown upon the planet, I must define his tones in terms of compassion and infinite love.

"Don't say any more, old man. It is terribly sad – but let us forget it."

No more was said, and we made preparations for our visit to the scene of industry.

An electric lift conveyed us to the top of the house, where we found upon the flat roof an air machine in waiting. Another moment and we ascended gently into the air. Ten minutes later we descended in a field adjacent to the works.

The works covered five hundred acres in all, and were the principal centre for the manufacture of domestic and agricultural requirements.

It was a busy scene into which we entered: and there were many points of similarity to that with which we were familiar. At the same time, having regard to the great contrast in the general economy of the planet, there were naturally many points of dissimilarity. Each worker followed a definite calling, the calling being a matter of choice, and choice being governed entirely by capacity. No misfits were possible under such a system, and from the lowest capacity to the highest, all were happy.

Being of terrestrial mould, I naturally enquired of Eueun the scale of pay. He gave me the answer that the scale of remuneration was every man's need. He therefore implied that as every man's need was more or less similar, irrespective of calling or status industrially, the remuneration was practically the same.

"But surely, Eueun, does that not tend to stymie individual enterprise?" I remonstrated. "At least," I added, "it would upon the Earth."

"Yes, I suppose it would upon the Earth," replied Eueun with a smile. "And I'll tell you why, Jim. Terrestrial dwellers cannot disassociate individual enterprise from self-aggrandisement. If one of your fellow inhabitants conceives an idea which, upon test, proves of great advantage to the community, he expects monetary reward and advancement of status."

"Well, so he should, seeing that it was his brain which has made the benefit possible to the community," I replied, countering Eueun's strange doctrine.

"But don't forget the terms I made use of, Jim," warned Eueun. "I used the terms 'monetary reward' and 'advancement of status'."

"And I still say that the individual who benefits the community should enjoy the rewards and honour of so doing," I answered.

"Then, in effect, Jim, you imply that the terms of which I made use and the terms used by yourself are synonymous?" Eueun queried.

"Yes!" I answered decidedly. "I certainly cannot disassociate them."

"*Cannot disassociate them?*" replied Eueun with equal emphasis. "Why, Jim... they are as opposite as the poles. 'Monetary reward' is grossly repugnant, and 'advancement of status' does nothing other than indicate a development of one's perceived greatness. But 'honour' is divine in its essence.

"Here upon Venus, every individual being makes use of the full capacity of brain for the benefit of the community. And the reward expected is the satisfaction of having done something in helping towards a more perfect life as a whole."

As we returned I felt considerably chastened. In pondering over what Eueun had said I realised he was right. At the same time I realised the poor old Earth was a long way from this ideal state of development.

And so we came to our last evening upon Venus. What would it mean to Paul? I felt very anxious about him.

Chapter 31

It is with great difficulty I set out to record the conclusion of our visit to Venus. We have been upon the return journey two days. I am seated at our cabin table, trying to write this chapter, but I almost feel like giving it up. If this record is ever published, I trust the reader will excuse the waywardness of the present chapter. My mind is in chaos. I cannot think coherently. I...

What is that? Paul's rousing! I must cease for a time.

I had to put down my pen a little while ago, in order to attend upon Paul. Poor old Paul. He was... But let me go back and follow in sequence.

Paul and Merna met on our last evening upon Venus. And such was the magnanimity of Mentor that they were left entirely alone. I have no idea of what occurred, but Eueun roused Sandy and I in the middle of the night to tell us we had better dress and proceed to the machine. Eueun informed us, to our dismay, that Paul was unconscious. It appears that Paul had become so violent that Mentor had to hypnotise him, and then drug him.

No word was spoken as we embarked in Eueun's aerodecker. Mentor and Eueun accompanied us, having first carried Paul on board.

It was breaking daylight when we arrived at the machine, and an inspection of the interior revealed that our friends had indeed made every provision for a comfortable return journey.

Our leave taking was to me poignant in the extreme. Sandy, for some inscrutable reason, was the antithesis of sadness. The grip of his hand to Eueun and Mentor was strong and confident. To both he made use of a strange and inexplicable formula.

"Mentor, Eueun," said he, with a thrill in his voice, "I understand now, and I am happy. I shall just wait for the time appointed. And then, and then…"

"Yes, and then?" queried Mentor, with a smile.

"Then will come my supreme happiness," answered Sandy.

"But, Mentor," continued Sandy, "deal gently with him who tried to harm me. Oh, how I trust he will soon commence his development towards goodness."

"He is surrounded by good influences, my young friend," replied Mentor gently. "And he will develop in time."

I did not understand the purport of their conversation at the time. Afterwards, it was made clear to me. That wonderful revelation must be conveyed to you, my dear reader, in Sandy's own words.

As I took Eueun's hand in mine, I felt I should have choked.

"Eueun," said I, falteringly. "Farewell has come months before I anticipated it. Both you and Mentor have been kindness personified to us in our visit. For that kindness I want to thank you from my heart. There was so much we would like to have seen; so much more we would like to have known. Is it possible that we may visit Venus again? I…"

"It is possible you may visit us again in your machine," interrupted Mentor kindly. "Yet I must say it is very improbable. Of course, at physical dissolution, you must come here. But to come on a like visit to the present one is doubtful. But cheer up, Jim, the full revelation will come to you, even as it must come to all of your fellows.

"Do not worry about Paul. He will remain unconscious for two days, and when he awakes, you will find him quite normal."

With a quick grip of the hand, Sandy and I entered the machine. We secured the cover of the man-tunnel and then entered the chart room. In a few moments we were in the air and on our way back to the old Earth.

When once we had cleared the pull of Venus, we were safe for weeks to come. Then to me came reactions and, moodily, I flung myself down upon my bedding.

"That won't do, Jim!" said Sandy, kindly but firmly. "Even though our visit came to an abrupt end, you must admit that while it lasted, it was stirring and unique. We have been favoured beyond our wildest dreams. We have had an adventure unparalleled to human experience. Let that thought help you, old man, when you are inclined to feel bitter."

"That's all very well, Sandy," I replied, somewhat resentfully, for I was in no mood to be taken to task. "For some inexplicable reason, you seem to take things without the slightest regret. What has happened to make you feel so?

You have not seemed quite the same since the night of that last attack upon you. What has made you change?"

"I cannot tell you, old man," replied Sandy with a softened accent. "It is too sacred."

Sandy paused for a moment as though he weighed something in his mind.

"Jim," he called quietly, "your questions put a new train of thought in mind. I know you are writing the account of our visit to Venus, and I'll tell you what I'll do. As I told you a moment ago, I cannot speak to you of that wonderful revelation which came to me, but I will write it down so that it may be included in the journal. When Paul is himself again, I will borrow your note book and write down just what happened. Will that do, old son?"

"Yes, that will do splendid," I replied, roused out of my moodiness. "I am sorry to have given way as I did, but I feel sore at our untimely return."

When Paul regained consciousness, the first word upon his lips was the name of her whom he loved so passionately.

"Merna!" he cried, "Merna, darling! Where are you? Ah, I remember! He shall not keep you from me! Curse him! Curse..."

"Paul! Paul!" expostulated Sandy.

Then, seeing our old comrade sink back with ashen face, Sandy spoke more gently. "Paul, old man, come, rouse up. Jim and I are here with you. Take a sip of this, Paul. It will hearten you and help you to see things with clearer vision."

Paul pushed the proffered stimulant from him, and turned on his face with a groan of anguish.

"Oh, Sandy, I want her!" he groaned. "I want her more than life itself. God! How I want her – my Merna!"

Then there came to Paul a clear realisation of all that had taken place. He looked up with a flush upon his face.

"We are in the machine, are we not?" he queried huskily. "I have lost my darling – and lost you and Jim your happiness. How I wish I could die out of it all! Just die with my old materialistic beliefs still with me. Death – and complete oblivion!"

"Hush, Paul. Do not wish that," said Sandy, leaning towards him as a mother would bend towards her sick child. "You have not lost me my happiness, old friend. Thank God I have found it, never to lose it again. And Jim does not mind leaving Venus now. Do not let anything worry you, Paul. Just get back to your old happy self. And remember this: just as you have seen and known Merna, so you will see her and know her again."

Sandy's words evidently brought comfort to Paul, for he turned over upon his side and slept like a child.

It was some days before Paul referred to this matter again. When he did, he did it of his own free will.

"I had no idea of the seriousness of my action," he began, "until what proved to be my last interview with Merna.

"On the night of the wedding festivities, I found Merna and I gravitating towards each other as though we had been acquainted for months. It was with a natural grace she came to my arms, and when I kissed her I found, to my unspeakable joy, she responded to my caresses. No thought of harm entered my head. She was delightfully human, and I can honestly say that no woman has ever stirred me as did Merna.

"In the cool of the night we wandered round those beautiful gardens. Presently we came to a little lowered alcove, and we passed within.

"Dear little soul. How I loved her. No – I'll come to the last interview.

"She came to me with exquisite sweetness, and with no reproach. 'Dearest,' she said, 'take me in your arms just once – then I must go.'

"As I took her in my arms, I protested passionately she should not leave me. But gently yet firmly, Merna reiterated it must be so. 'I do not regret one moment of our ecstasy, Paul, but realisation has come to me. Our love must cost you an immediate return to the Earth. I, too, must pay forfeit, yet I say again, I do not regret what has taken place. I love you, Paul! Nay, seek not to detain me.'

"My arms apparently were still round her – but she was gone!

"I think I lost my senses then. Mentor came in and I cursed him. What happened after, I do not know. I awoke to find myself here in the machine.

"I know, now, the enormity of my crime. My Merna must suffer for my wrong. And Mentor, kindest of all friends, I have insulted."

The recital of this sad episode cost Paul more than we could estimate. Sandy told him gently of Mentor's entire forgiveness. And that Merna would again recover her former status upon Venus. But our old comrade was never quite the same afterwards.

I must now leave to Sandy the recital of his own story.

Chapter 32

To the reader of this journal:

The chronicler of this journal has led you, step by step, through the whole of our adventures upon the planet Venus. One experience alone has he omitted. That one experience falls to my lot to recount. It is fitting that I should recount it – because it is a personal experience.

My friend has already told you of the bitter-sweet memory of my dear wife. She was a cripple, but in God's good mercy, she was completely restored to health. For three wonderful years, she brought sunshine to my life. Then came darkness. She, the most beautiful creature on God's Earth, lay at my feet, battered out of recognition.

I was waiting upon the platform for my darling, she having gone to some friends for a short holiday. I heard the sickening crash but five hundred yards outside the station. Scarcely knowing what I did, I hurried to the spot. And there, amidst the wreckage, I found her.

As I looked upon her and slowly realised I should never again hear her dear voice, never again find her thrill under my caresses, I think I went near mad. I felt I had lost my all. I gave up writing (I was engaged upon a book at the time) and became a wanderer.

In process of time I came in contact with Paul and Jim, along with the late Christopher Jackson, whose journey to the Moon has already been recorded. Contact with my dear old chums opened up a new avenue of interest. Soon we were busily engaged in constructing Mr Jackson's machine, and gradually the aches became less poignant.

Then came our project to Venus, opening up, as it did, the prelude to my wonderful revelation.

When the startling news came to us that an invisible passenger was journeying with us in the machine, I certainly did not at first connect it with my dear wife's presence. But when Paul told us of his strange adventure upon that memorable night, and his description of who had conversed with him, I knew at once it was none other but my sweetheart.

It hurt me considerably at the time that Paul should see her and converse with her, while my heart was hungering for her. But when I realised the significance of that manifestation – that it came to change Paul from his materialism to a firm faith – I no longer felt resentment. Rather, I rejoiced that the influence of my darling had produced such a change.

How I longed to see her! Day after day and night after night I waited, ever praying that a sight of her whom I still loved with unabated strength may be granted me. But, to my sorrow, no sight came.

Then came that time of horror when we were adjusting the atmospheres between that of Venus and our machine. I heard my beloved's name spoken, and instinctively realised it was spoken by vile lips. I turned in wonder to see who could be with me in the man-tunnel, for I knew Paul and Jim had gone to the chart-room. I could see no one, but instantly I was seized by invisible hands. Struggle as I could, I made no impression upon that horrible menace. A vibratory bubble seemed to set about me and it said:

"Curse you, mortal! Curse you! You shall never have her. I will kill you first, and afterwards damn you to eternal disappointment!"

My friend has told you in the journal how I was rescued by Paul and himself, and how, at last, I recovered from the shock of the experience. It came to me clearly that the invisible menace was trying to prevent me seeing my darling. After that, I felt more confident I would see her before I left the planet. Later this conviction was strengthened by both Mentor and Eueun.

And then came the memorable night in which full revelation came. I may say that this wonderful revelation completely changed my life.

When I retired for the night, I had scarcely relaxed for sleep when I was again attacked by that awful menace. Eueun rescued me from that tenacious hold, but the shock of contact rendered me unconscious. Eueun and Jim remained with me until I had recovered, and then, under Eueun's permission, I sank into a deep sleep.

I have no idea how long I slept, but suddenly I was awakened with my nerves a-tingle.

A soft light cast its radiance around the room, and though I knew it was not daylight, I hastily donned my clothes. And then (shall I ever forget it?), a well-loved voice was singing. I knew the voice. I knew the song. I had composed that song during the delights of our honeymoon; a song my darling only used to sing.

"Sweetheart!" I cried, in an agony of pent-up rapture. "Oh, God! Where are you?"

Softly and lingeringly came the reply: "I am here, dearest. Here with you."

The scales fell from my eyes. And there before me... was my darling.

She was beautiful upon Earth. But now... how can I describe her? I cannot. Mere words would detract from her glorious beauty. That memory must be mine alone. So wondrous was the purity of her loveliness, that, though joy surged through my being, I feared to approach her. Swiftly she came to me. She was in my arms with her dear arms around my neck.

"Jock, dearest," said she, using the name by which she had ever known me. "At last I can make myself known to you. I have so much wanted to do this, not merely to strengthen your faith, but more to chase away the sorrow you have felt since I left you in the physical sense. Really, I have never left you. I have ever been near you, trying to influence you against your grief."

"Yes, my darling," I answered, holding her close to me. "I have felt you near me, many times. I knew by the love which bound us that the grave could not hold you there. I felt that you were free: free and buoyant as the ether which surrounds the planets. But I am only human and I could not overcome my sorrow."

"Ah, Jock," said my wife, and her voice was infinitely sweet and tender. "If the people of Earth only realised the peace and bliss of their loved ones, and how near they were to them, they would never grieve or sorrow. It is because they do not realise this that they sorrow. Always remember, dearest, we are never, never lost to our loved ones."

It was infinitely sweet to have my dear wife near me once more, and to look into her loving eyes. All the bitterness and resentment vanished as mist vanishes before the sun. How I wished I could remain upon Venus and never return to the Earth. My wife must have sensed my thoughts, for she said: "You must not wish to remain upon Venus, Jock. You will return to the Earth to-morrow, for you have much work to do there. I want you to devote the remaining years of your life upon Earth in teaching the great truths you have been taught here.

"The supreme Love of the Master of the Spheres. The grand vista which opens to all who pass through the gateway of physical death.

"That every encouragement is given to those who are vile to become good, and that the doctrine of one becoming 'lost' is wrong and meaningless. And dearest, when you, too, have passed through that gateway, I shall be here waiting for you."

"Will it be soon?" I asked, eagerly.

"Ah, no dear! You must not wish to come soon. Let your work upon Earth be first performed. I shall be near you ever to help. And help poor Paul. He will need your sympathy. Tell him I will look after Merna."

I cannot tell the reader more. Our leave-taking was too sacred for record. This only will I say. All my grief has gone. It is lost in the wonderful revelation of Love. I feel my darling ever near me. And when I return to the Earth, God helping me, I shall carry out her behest.

Herewith, I conclude my brief contribution to this journal and subscribe myself, Sandy.

* * *

It is left to me to conclude the journal. I have read through Sandy's contribution, and it has brought me much comfort. No vision has been granted me, yet I am happy in the knowledge of truth as given to Sandy. I intend to suggest to him, presently, that I have the honour of helping him in the glorious work set before him.

We have now been upon the return journey for five months. No adventure has befallen us, and we are looking forward to a safe and successful landing home. Paul has recovered greatly from his depression, and I trust that he, too, will join forces in the great work ahead.

I fear it is very improbable that we shall visit Venus again. The great work imposed upon Sandy will prevent this, I think. But if at any time we should seek further adventures, I shall certainly record them. Until then, farewell!

—— The End ——

Concluding Note by GEH

It is very certain that our three adventurers landed in perfect safety, otherwise I should not be in possession of their journal. I do not know where they now are. If, at any time, they venture upon further discoveries, I trust I may be the fortunate individual to receive their records. If this should be my lot, I promise to deal as faithfully with their next venture as I have endeavoured to do with the present one. I also hope that no unfortunate circumstance may curtail their fortunes as it did in the Visit to Venus.

Postscript

There are many reasons to regret the untimely death of George Hobbs in December 1946, aged just 63.

However, it is particularly poignant that, had George lived to a riper old age, then he would have seen events unfold that would undoubtedly have thrilled him: the first man in space (1961) and the first man on the moon (1969). But these are events that he might have considered inevitable, whereas the role that his home town of Swindon would play in space exploration would have been harder to predict, but no less thrilling.

The headquarters of the British National Space Centre (BNSC), an executive government agency that co-ordinated civil space activity in the UK, were at Polaris House, North Star Avenue, Swindon, from January 2009, and soon after (from April 1, 2010), it was replaced by the United Kingdom Space Agency (UKSA) at the same location.

An agency of the Department for Business, Energy & Industrial Strategy, the UKSA has a staff of around 260, based in Swindon, London and Harwell, Oxfordshire, www.gov.uk/government/organisations/uk-space-agency stating that its purpose is to 'inspire and lead the UK in space, to benefit our planet and its people'.

The website confirms its responsibilities as: providing technical advice on Government space strategy; guiding the UK space sector to deliver the Government's vision; designing and delivering programmes that implement Government strategy, including as a sponsor of national capabilities and an early-stage investor in space research and development; promoting the UK space sector's interests and achievements; making connections to join up industry and academia; and representing the UK in international space programmes.

Such programmes include the Esa-Nasa Solar Orbiter and the Esa-Jaxa BepiColombo missions – two projects that, separated by a single day in August 2021 (while this book was being prepared for publication), were making *a visit to Venus.*

Acknowledgements

Noel Ponting & Graham Carter would like to extend a big thank-you to the following for their help and support in relation to this book:

Newsquest Media Group Ltd,
Shannon Jones, Dr Julie Miller, Emma Ponting, Lydia Ponting,
Peter Field, Tom Field

So-called 'ordinary' working towns sometimes hide their lights under bushels, *A Swindon Wordsmith* aimed to put the record straight to some extent – by paying tribute to one of the town's forgotten writers.

George Ewart Hobbs deserves to be remembered alongside fellow Swindon writers Alfred Williams and Richard Jefferies, particularly as his works tell us so much about the times through which he lived (1883-1946).

Despite working full-time, for more than half a century, as a Great Western Railway engineer, George was a prolific writer, most of his works commissioned as weekly columns in the *Swindon Advertiser*.

For the first time, this book republishes a sample of his works, including articles about many of the subjects that fascinated him – religion, philosophy, astronomy, spiritualism, engineering and more. But it also includes poetry, eyewitness reports on remarkable events of the day, pioneering comic sketches and even science fiction stories.

As well as this literary legacy, Hobbs's vivid writing provides us with a unique and brilliantly observed insight into everyday and so-called 'ordinary' life in Swindon, a century ago.

A Swindon Radical is a book that was never intended. After all, when its predecessor, *A Swindon Wordsmith*, was published in 2019, highlighting the life and works of railwayman and part-time writer George Ewart Hobbs, the authors were satisfied that it achieved both of their main aims, showcasing work by someone who had undeservedly been forgotten since his death in 1946, but also opening a fascinating window on bygone Swindon.

However, the surprise discovery of more works by George made it necessary to produce a second volume, and this book therefore samples some of the articles he wrote and published in the 1920s and 1930s, mostly in the *Swindon Advertiser*.

Like *A Swindon Wordsmith*, this new book covers a wide range of George's interests, including religion, philosophy, astronomy, spiritualism, engineering and more.

And as he came to terms with a changing world at home and as the world spiralled towards the second declaration of global war in his lifetime, it chronicles the views of an increasingly radical thinker, who was always ahead of his time.

Along with a simultaneously published companion book, *A Visit to Venus*, *A Swindon Radical* completes the story of this fascinating wordsmith and free-thinker.

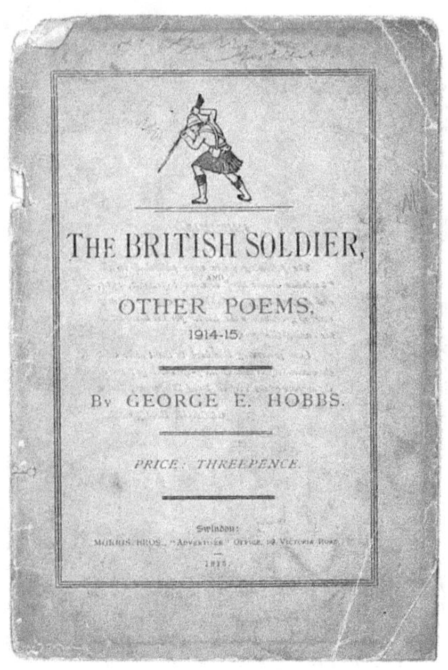
THE BRITISH SOLDIER,
AND
OTHER POEMS,
1914-15.
By GEORGE E. HOBBS.
PRICE: THREEPENCE.
Swindon:

The first (and until *A Swindon Wordsmith* and *A Swindon Radical* the only) anthology of George Hobbs's work to be published was *The British Soldier and Other Poems 1914-15*.

Morris Bros, publishers of the *Swindon Advertiser*, produced the booklet, which contained 24 poems, 23 of which had appeared in the paper during the period October 1914 to July 1915.

It is now extremely rare, but readers may obtain a PDF of it by emailing shresearch2@gmail.com.

www.ingramcontent.com/pod-product-compliance
Lightning Source LLC
LaVergne TN
LVHW020055110826
845155LV00022B/86

* 9 7 8 1 9 1 4 4 0 7 2 2 2 *